William Shakespeare's Julius Caesar: A Retelling in Prose

David Bruce

Published by David Bruce, 2022.

WILLIAM SHAKESPEARE'S JULIUS CAESAR: A RETELLING IN PROSE

First edition. July 26, 2022.

Copyright © 2022 David Bruce.

ISBN: 979-8201192525

Written by David Bruce.

Table of Contents

Dedication

Dedicated to Carl Eugene Bruce and Josephine Saturday Bruce

My father, Carl Eugene Bruce, died on 24 October 2013. He used to work for Ohio Power, and at one time, his job was to shut off the electricity of people who had not paid their bills. He sometimes would find a home with an impoverished mother and some children. Instead of shutting off their electricity, he would tell the mother that she needed to pay her bill or soon her electricity would be shut off. He would write on a form that no one was home when he stopped by because if no one was home he did not have to shut off their electricity.

The best good deed that anyone ever did for my father occurred after a storm that knocked down many power lines. He and other linemen worked long hours and got wet and cold. Their feet were freezing because water got into their boots and soaked their socks. Fortunately, a kind woman gave my father and the other linemen dry socks to wear.

My mother, Josephine Saturday Bruce, died on 14 June 2003. She used to work at a store that sold clothing. One day, an impoverished mother with a baby clothed in rags walked into the store and started shoplifting in an interesting way: The mother took the rags off her baby and dressed the infant in new clothing. My mother knew that this mother could not afford to buy the clothing, but she helped the mother dress her baby and then she watched as the mother walked out of the store without paying.

***

The doing of good deeds is important. As a free person, you can choose to live your life as a good person or as a bad person. To be a good person, do good deeds. To be a bad person, do bad deeds. If you do good deeds, you will become good. If you do bad deeds, you will become bad. To become the person you want to be, act as if you already are that kind of person. Each of us chooses what kind of person we will become. To become a good person, do the things a good person does. To become a bad person, do the things a bad person does. The opportunity to take action to become the kind of person you want to be is yours.

A Buddhist monk visiting a class wrote this on the chalkboard: "EVERYONE WANTS TO SAVE THE WORLD, BUT NO ONE

WANTS TO HELP MOM DO THE DISHES." The students laughed, but the monk then said, "Statistically, it's highly unlikely that any of you will ever have the opportunity to run into a burning orphanage and rescue an infant. But, in the smallest gesture of kindness — a warm smile, holding the door for the person behind you, shoveling the driveway of the elderly person next door — you have committed an act of immeasurable profundity, because to each of us, our life is our universe."

Educate Yourself
Read Like A Wolf Eats
Be Excellent to Each Other
Books Then, Books Now, Books Forever

***

In this retelling, as in all my retellings, I have tried to make the work of literature accessible to modern readers who may lack some of the knowledge about mythology, religion, and history that the literary work's contemporary audience had.

Do you know a language other than English? If you do, I give you permission to translate this book, copyright your translation, publish or self-publish it, and keep all the royalties for yourself. (Do give me credit, of course, for the original retelling.)

I would like to see my retellings of classic literature used in schools, so I give permission to the country of Finland (and all other countries) to give copies of this book to all students forever. I also give permission to the state of Texas (and all other states) to give copies of this book to all students forever. I also give permission to all teachers to give copies of this book to all students forever.

Teachers need not actually teach my retellings. Teachers are welcome to give students copies of my books as background material. For example, if they are teaching Homer's *Iliad* and *Odyssey*, teachers are welcome to give students copies of my *Virgil's* Aeneid: *A Retelling in Prose* and tell students, "Here's another ancient epic you may want to read in your spare time."

PREFACE

For hundreds of years, the Romans had a republic rather than a kingdom. Many influential Romans, however, were afraid that Julius Caesar wanted to be King of the Romans, and they were determined to stop him. Shakespeare's play tells what happened to Caesar and to those people who conspired against him.

CAST OF CHARACTERS

Male Characters

Julius Caesar

Octavius Caesar, Marcus Antonius, M. Aemilius Lepidus, triumvirs after the death of Julius Caesar

Cicero, Publius, Popilius Lena, Senators

Marcus Brutus, Caius Cassius, Casca, Trebonius, Ligarius, Decius Brutus, Metellus Cimber, Cinna, conspirators against Julius Caesar

Flavius and Marullus, tribunes

Artemidorus, a sophist of Cnidos

A Soothsayer

Cinna, a poet

Another Poet

Lucilius, Titinius, Messala, Young Cato, Volumnius, friends to Brutus and Cassius

Varro, Clitus, Claudius, Strato, Lucius, Dardanius, servants to Brutus

Pindarus, servant to Cassius

Female Characters

Calpurnia, wife to Caesar

Portia, wife to Brutus

Minor Characters

Commoners, or Plebeians, of Rome; Senators, Guards, Attendants, etc.

CHAPTER 1

— 1.1 —

On a street in Rome, some skilled workers, including a carpenter and a cobbler, were celebrating the triumphal procession of Julius Caesar, who had defeated his political rival, Pompey, and Pompey's two sons, in a civil war. Now Julius Caesar held the power in Rome, and some Roman citizens worried that he wanted to be King. To be King, he would have to do away with the Roman Republic.

Two Roman tribunes named Flavius and Marullus arrived. They were angry at the commoners for celebrating Julius Caesar's victory.

Flavius said to the commoners, "Get away from here! Go home, you idle creatures, go home! Is this a holiday? Don't you mechanicals — you laborers — know that you ought not walk on these streets on a work day unless you are wearing work clothes and carrying the tools of your profession?"

He asked one of the laborers, "Tell me, what is your trade?"

"Why, sir, I am a carpenter."

Marullus said to him, "Where are your leather apron and your ruler? Why are you wearing your best clothing?"

He asked another laborer, "You, sir, what trade do you follow?"

"Truly, sir, compared to a fine workman, I am only, as you would say, a cobbler."

Marullus misheard him: "A bungler? No doubt. But what trade do you follow?"

The cobbler, who was in a joking mood, replied, "A trade, sir, that I hope I may practice with a safe conscience. I am indeed, sir, a mender of bad soles."

Marullus, understanding this to mean that the person repaired bad souls, asked again, "What trade do you follow, you knave? You worthless knave, what trade do you follow?"

The cobbler replied, "Sir, please do not be out with me, but if you are out, sir, I can mend you."

The cobbler smiled, thinking, *That was a good joke: "Sir, please do not be out of patience with me, but if you are out of shoes — that is, if your shoes are worn out — sir, I can mend you — that is, I can mend your shoes or I can improve your character."*

Marullus, who did not understand the joke, said, "What do you mean by that? What do you mean by 'mend me,' you saucy fellow!"

"Why, sir, I can cobble you."

Flavius interrupted, "So you are a cobbler, are you?"

"Truly, sir, I make my living by using the awl to pierce holes. I meddle with no tradesman's matters, nor women's matters, except with an awl to pierce holes."

The cobbler smiled, thinking, *That is another good joke. I use a tool like an awl to pierce a woman's hole.*

He added, "I am, indeed, sir, a surgeon to old shoes; when they are in great danger, I recover — that is, repair — them. As proper men as have ever trod upon cowhide have trod upon my handiwork — many men of standing have trod the ground while wearing my shoes."

Flavius asked, "But why aren't you working in your shop today? Why are you leading these men about the streets?"

The cobbler joked, "Truly, sir, I am trying to wear out their shoes, to get myself more work. But, indeed, sir, we are taking a holiday today so that we can see Julius Caesar and rejoice in his triumph."

Marullus said, "What is there to rejoice at? What conquest of foreign foes has he made? What captured enemies has he brought to Rome to be displayed in captive bonds beside his chariot-wheels? You blocks, you stones, you worse than senseless things! You hard hearts, you cruel men of Rome — don't you remember Pompey? You used to often climb up on walls and battlements, climb up towers and look out windows, and climb chimney-tops, with your infants in your arms, and there you used to sit the entire day, with patient expectation, to see great Pompey pass through the streets of Rome. When you saw his chariot appear, you used to shout all together and make the Tiber River tremble underneath her banks as your shouts echoed along its overhanging riverbanks. And now you put on your best clothing? And now you call this a holiday? And now you strew flowers in the way of the man who comes in triumph over Pompey's blood? Caesar defeated and killed Pompey's two sons. You workmen, go away from here! Run to your houses, fall upon your knees, and pray to the gods to hold back the plague that ought to come to punish this ingratitude."

Flavius said, "Go, go, good countrymen, and, to expiate this fault of yours, assemble all the poor men of your sort, take them to the banks of the Tiber River, and weep your tears into the river until the lowest part of the stream rises up to the highest riverbanks."

The commoners departed.

Flavius said to Marullus, "The commoners seem to be moved in the right way — they vanish tongue-tied in their guiltiness. You go down that way towards the Capitol — the temple of Jupiter on the Capitoline Hill — and I will go this way. If you see any statues decorated with Caesar's trophies, strip them."

Marullus asked, "May we do so? You know it is the Feast of Lupercal. Now is when we hold a feast day to honor the fertility god Lupercus. Won't it be sacrilegious to strip the statues?"

Flavius replied, "It doesn't matter. Let no statues be hung with Caesar's trophies — with decorations to honor Julius Caesar. I will go around and drive away the commoners from the streets. You do the same thing when you see many commoners gathered together. We need to restrain these early signs of enthusiasm for Caesar. That will keep him from flying so high above us that we will all feel servile and fearful. If we can pluck some of his feathers now, we can keep him from flying high above us."

— 1.2 —

In a public place in Rome were standing Julius Caesar, Calpurnia (Caesar's wife), Brutus, Portia (Brutus' wife), Mark Antony, Decius Brutus, Cicero, Caius Cassius, and Casca. A great crowd of people, among them a soothsayer (fortune teller), were around them. Trumpets occasionally sounded. Marullus and Flavius now came walking up to the group of people; they had arrived too late to keep the commoners from gathering around Caesar.

Caesar said, "Calpurnia!"

Casca ordered, "Everyone, be quiet. Caesar is speaking."

Caesar said again, "Calpurnia!"

Calpurnia replied, "Here I am, my lord."

"Mark Antony will be one of the young men running naked through the streets and touching spectators with leather thongs to celebrate the Feast of

Lupercal," Caesar said. "Make sure that you stand directly in Mark Antony's way when he runs."

He then called, "Antony!"

"Yes, my lord."

"Do not forget when you are running naked through the streets to touch Calpurnia because our wise men say that barren women, when touched in this holy chase, will be cured of the curse of sterility."

"I shall remember to do so," Antony replied. "When Caesar says, 'Do this,' it will be done."

"Let us proceed," Caesar said. "We will observe all the rites."

The soothsayer in the crowd called, "Caesar!"

"Who is calling me?" Caesar asked.

Casca ordered, "Let all noise stop. Again, be quiet!"

"Who in the press of people is calling my name? I hear a voice, shriller than all the music, crying, 'Caesar!' Speak to me. Caesar is ready to listen to you."

The soothsayer called, "Beware the Ides of March — beware March 15."

"Which man is saying that?" Caesar asked.

One of Caesar's friends, Brutus, replied, "A soothsayer tells you to beware the Ides of March."

"Set him before me; let me see his face."

"Soothsayer, come from the crowd," Cassius said. "Look at Caesar."

"What have you to say to me now?" Caesar asked. "Speak once again."

"Beware the Ides of March."

"He is a dreamer," Caesar said. "Let us leave him. Let us pass him."

Everyone departed except for Brutus and Cassius. The two men were brothers-in-law. Cassius was married to one of Brutus' three sisters.

Cassius asked Brutus, "Will you go and see the progress of the race?"

"No," Brutus replied.

"Please, do so."

"I am not a merry fellow who is fond of games," Brutus said. "I lack the quick and lively spirit that Mark Antony has in abundance. But do not let me stop you from enjoying the race, Cassius."

"Brutus, I have lately been observing you. You no longer look at me with that gentleness and show of friendship that you used to have for me. You are intent on having your own way, and you are treating me less than as a friend although I still love and respect you."

"Cassius, do not be deceived. If I have veiled my face and not shown my true feelings, I do so because I turn my troubled looks only upon myself. Recently, I have been vexed with greatly conflicting emotions that concern only myself. This perhaps has changed my behavior. But my good friends should not therefore grieve — and I count you, Cassius, among my good friends. Do not interpret my neglect of my friends as meaning anything more than that I am at war with myself and therefore I forget to show my friendship to my friends."

"Then, Brutus, I have much misunderstood your feelings. Because of that, I have not told you certain important thoughts of great value — they are worthy cogitations. Tell me, good Brutus, can you see your own face?"

"No, Cassius, I cannot. The eye cannot see itself unless it is reflected by something such as a mirror or a calm surface of water."

"That is true, and it is very much to be lamented, Brutus, that you have no such mirrors as will reflect your hidden worthiness to your eye, so that you might see your reflection. I have heard many people of the highest importance in Rome, except for immortal Caesar, speak about you and wish that noble Brutus could see what they see."

"Into what dangers are you trying to lead me, Cassius, that you want me to seek within myself for qualities that are not in me?"

"Good Brutus, listen to me. Since you know that the best way to see yourself is by reflection, I will be your mirror and without exaggeration reveal to yourself things about yourself that you do not know. Do not be suspicious of me, noble Brutus. Regard me as dangerous if you know that I am a common laughingstock, or if you know that I am accustomed to cheapen my friendship by promising it with clichéd oaths to every new person who comes along, or if you know that I pretend to be friends with men and hug them hard and afterwards slander them, or if you know that I make professions of friendship to everyone after I have had a few drinks."

A great shout arose in the distance.

"What does this shouting mean?" Brutus asked. "I am afraid that the Roman people have chosen Caesar to be their King."

"Are you afraid of that?" Cassius asked. "Then I have to think that you do not want Julius Caesar to be King."

"I do not want Caesar to be King, Cassius, although I love and respect Caesar. But why are you keeping me here so long? What is it that you want to say to me? If you want me to do something for the general good — the public welfare — then I would do it even if it meant that I would die. I pray that the gods help me only as long as I love the name of honor more than I fear death."

"I know that virtue is in you, Brutus, as well as I know your outward appearance," Cassius said. "Honor is what I want to talk to you about. I cannot tell what you and other men think about this life, but speaking for myself, I would rather be dead than live in awe of someone who is just a man like myself. I was born as free as Caesar; so were you. We both have eaten as well as Caesar, and we both can endure the winter's cold as well as he. I remember that once, on a raw and gusty day, when the troubled Tiber River was raging against the restraint of her banks, Caesar said to me, 'Do you dare, Cassius, to now leap in with me into this angry flood, and swim to that point over there?' Hearing that, fully dressed as I was, I plunged in and bade him to follow me. He also jumped into the river. The torrent roared, and we fought against it with strong arms, throwing it aside and making progress and competing against each other and the river. But before we could arrive at the point that Caesar had proposed, he cried, 'Help me, Cassius, or I will sink and drown!' Aeneas, our great ancestor, had put his aged father upon his shoulder and carried him away from the flames of Troy. I did the same thing: I put the tired Caesar upon my shoulder and carried him out of the Tiber River. And this man — Caesar — has now become a god, and Cassius is only a wretched creature who must bend his body and bow whenever Caesar carelessly nods at him. Caesar had a fever when he was in Spain, and when the fit was on him, I noticed how he shook. It is true: This god did shake. He went pale, color fled from his coward lips, and that same eye whose glance awes the world lost its luster. I heard him groan — indeed, I did — and that tongue of his that makes the Romans take notice of him and even copy his speeches into their books cried, 'Give me something to drink, Titinius,' as if he were a sick girl. By the gods, it amazes me that a man of such a feeble constitution has outraced the world and seized power and carried away the victor's crown of palm leaves."

The crowd of people around Caesar shouted again.

"I hear another great shout!" Brutus said. "I do believe that these shouts are for some new honors that are heaped on Caesar."

"Caesar straddles the world like the Colossus of Rhodes — a huge statue that is said to have spanned the entrance to the harbor of the Greek island of Rhodes," Cassius said. "We petty men walk under Caesar's huge legs and peep about and find ourselves dishonorable graves. Men at some time are masters of their fates: The fault, dear Brutus, is not in our stars, but in ourselves, if we find that we are only underlings.

"Think of the names Brutus and Caesar. What is special about that 'Caesar'? Why should that name be sounded more than yours? Write them together. Your name is as fair a name as his name. Say the two names. Your name fills the mouth as well as his name. Weigh the two names. Your name is as heavy as his name. Conjure up spirits with the two names. The name 'Brutus' will raise a spirit as quickly as will the name 'Caesar.'

"Now, in the names of all the gods at once, what meat has this Caesar eaten that he is grown so great? Our era should be ashamed! Rome, you have lost the breed of noble-blooded men! You are not raising men of notable worth! Since the great flood that Zeus, King of gods and men, sent to punish Humankind — a great flood that only one man and only one woman survived — when has there ever been an era in which only one man was considered great! When could people say until now, when they talked about Rome, that her wide walls contained only one man? Now Rome indeed has plenty of room, because only one man is in it.

"You and I have heard our fathers say that there was a Brutus once who would have allowed the eternal devil to rule Rome exactly as much as he would have allowed a King to rule Rome!"

Cassius was referring to an ancestor of Brutus — Lucius Junius Brutus — who had driven the last King out of Rome in the 6th century BCE and had founded the Roman Republic.

Brutus replied, "That you do love and respect me, I have no doubt. What you would persuade me to do, I have some idea. How I have thought of this and of these times, I shall tell you at a later time; at present, I will not, so respectfully I ask you not to try to persuade me to do anything. I will think about what you have said. What you have to say to me later, I will patiently listen to, and I will find a suitable time when we can meet and discuss such important matters.

"Until then, my noble friend, think about this: Brutus would prefer to be a villager than to be known as a son of Rome under the hard conditions that this time is likely to lay upon us."

"I am glad that my weak words have struck even this much show of fire from Brutus," Cassius said.

"The games are done and Caesar is returning," Brutus said.

"As Caesar and the others walk by us, grab Casca's sleeve," Cassius said. "He will, after his sour fashion, tell you what has happened that is worthy of note today."

Caesar and his band of followers walked toward Brutus and Cassius.

"I will do as you say," Brutus said. "But, look, Cassius, an angry spot glows on Caesar's brow, and all the rest look like they have been scolded. Calpurnia's cheek is pale; and Cicero looks around with fiery and angry eyes like a ferret hunting rats. We have seen him look this way in the Capitol after some Senators have opposed him in debate."

"Casca will tell us what has happened."

Caesar said, "Antony!"

"Caesar?" Antony answered.

"Let me have men about me who are fat, who smoothly comb their hair, and who sleep throughout the night. Cassius over there has a lean and hungry look; he thinks too much. Such men are dangerous."

"Do not fear him," Antony said. "He is not dangerous. He is a noble Roman and has a good reputation."

"I wish that he were fatter!" Julius Caesar replied. "But I do not fear him. Yet if I had any tendency to be afraid, I do not know the man I would avoid as quickly as that lean Cassius. He reads much. He is a great observer, and he looks at the deeds of men and understands the men's motives. He does not love to watch plays the way that you do, Antony. He does not listen to music. He seldom smiles, and when he does smile, he smiles as if he is mocking himself because he is smiling at something. Such men as he are never comfortable when they see a greater man than themselves, and therefore they are very dangerous.

"I am telling you what ought to be feared rather than what I fear; for always I am Caesar and I am afraid of nothing.

"Come over to my right side because my left ear is deaf, and tell me truly what you think about Cassius."

Everybody left except for Brutus, Cassius, and Casca, who said to Brutus, "You pulled me by my cloak. Do you want to speak to me?"

"Yes, Casca. Tell us what happened just now. Why does Caesar look so serious?"

"Why, you were with him, weren't you?"

Brutus replied, "If I had been with him, I would not now be asking you what happened."

"Why, the crown of a King was offered to Caesar, who pushed it away with the back of his hand, and then people began to shout."

"What was the second shout we heard for?"

"Why, that was for the same reason. Caesar was offered the crown a second time."

Cassius said, "The people shouted three times. What was the last cry for?"

"Why, for that same reason, too."

Brutus asked, "Was the Kingly crown offered to Caesar three times?"

"Yes, it was," Casca answered. "Caesar pushed it away three times, each time gentler than the previous time. Each time he pushed it away, the crowd of respectable people around me shouted."

Cassius asked, "Who offered Caesar the crown?"

"Why, Antony," Casca replied.

"Tell us how everything happened, noble Casca," Brutus requested.

"I can as well be hanged as tell you how it happened," Casca said. "It was mere foolery, and so I did not pay attention to it. I saw Mark Antony offer Caesar a crown — and yet it was not a crown — it was one of these coronets. As I told you, Caesar pushed it away the first time Antony offered it to him — but, for all that, I think that Caesar wanted to have it. Then Antony offered it to him again, and again Caesar pushed it away — and again I think that he hated to let go of it. And then Antony offered it the third time, and Caesar pushed it away the third time. Each time he refused the crown, the rabble hooted and clapped their chapped hands and threw into the air their sweaty caps and breathed out a huge amount of stinking breath because Caesar refused the crown. Their stinking breath almost choked Caesar — he fainted and fell down at it. As for myself, I dared not laugh for fear of opening my lips and breathing in the bad air."

"Did you say that Caesar fainted?" Cassius asked.

"He fell down in the marketplace, and foamed at the mouth, and was speechless."

"It is very likely that he has the falling sickness — epilepsy," Brutus said.

Cassius said, "No, Caesar does not have the falling sickness, but you and I and honest Casca, we have the falling sickness. We have fallen."

"I do not know what you mean by that, but I am sure that Caesar fell down," Casca said. "If the rag-tag people did not applaud him and hiss him, accordingly as he pleased or displeased them, as they are accustomed to treat the actors in the theater, I am no true man."

"What did Caesar say when he regained consciousness?" Brutus asked.

"Before he fell down, when he perceived that the common herd was glad that he refused the crown, he opened his jacket and offered them his throat to cut. If I had been a common laborer, I wish I would go to Hell among the rogues if I had not taken him at his word. If I had been a common laborer, I would have cut his throat. Caesar fell then. When he came to himself again, he said that if he had done or said anything amiss, he wanted the crowd of people to think it was because of his infirmity. Three or four young women who were standing near me cried, 'Alas, good soul!' and forgave him with all their hearts, but we do not need to pay any attention to them. If Caesar had stabbed their mothers, they would have done the same thing."

"And after that, he went away, sad and serious?" Brutus asked.

"Yes."

"Did Cicero say anything?" Cassius asked.

"Yes, he spoke Greek."

"To what purpose? What was the content of what he said?"

"I don't know. If I could tell you that, I would never look you again in the face; however, those who understood Greek smiled at one another and shook their heads. As for myself, it was Greek to me and I did not understand it. But I can tell you some news: Marullus and Flavius, because they pulled decorations off the statues of Caesar, have been deprived of their positions as Tribunes who speak for the people — they have been silenced. Farewell. There was more foolery, if I could remember it."

"Will you eat with me tonight, Casca?" Cassius asked.

"No, I have promised to eat with someone else."

"Will you dine with me tomorrow?"

"Yes, if I am still alive and you haven't changed your mind and your dinner is worth eating."

"Good. I will expect you tomorrow."

"Do so. Farewell, both of you."

He left.

"What a blunt fellow has Casca grown to be!" Brutus said. "He had a quick mind when he was going to school."

"He still has a quick mind when it comes to taking action in any bold or noble enterprise," Cassius said. "However, he pretends to be insensitive and careless. This rudeness of his is a sauce to his good intelligence; it gives men the stomach to digest his words with better appetite."

"You know him well," Brutus said. "At this time I will leave you. Tomorrow, if you want to speak with me, I will go to your house, or, if you prefer, you can come to my house. I will stay there until you come."

"I will come to your house tomorrow," Cassius said. "Until then, think of the state of the world."

Brutus left.

Cassius said to himself, "Well, Brutus, you are noble, yet I see that your honorable metal and mettle may be bent into a new shape. Because such a thing can happen, it is fitting that noble minds keep company always with other noble minds because who is so firm and incorruptible that he cannot be seduced and corrupted? Caesar has a grudge against me and barely tolerates my presence, but he loves and respects Brutus. If I were Brutus and he were Cassius, he would not be able to manipulate me. I will this night throw through his windows several letters, written in different kinds of handwriting so that they look like they have come from several citizens. The letters will testify to the great opinion that Roman citizens hold of you, Brutus, and your name. They will also hint at the ambition of Caesar. Soon, Caesar had better brace himself because we will shake him and undermine him or suffer the consequences of failure. If we do not stop Julius Caesar from becoming King, worse days will follow."

— 1.3 —

On a street in Rome, Casca, with his sword drawn, met Cicero. Thunder sounded and lightning flashed.

Cicero recognized Casca and said, "Good evening, Casca. Did you escort Caesar home? Why are you breathless? And why do you stare in that way?"

"Are you not moved when all the realm of the Earth shakes like a thing unsteady and insecure? Cicero, I have seen tempests when the scolding winds have split knotty oaks, and I have seen the ocean swell and rage and foam as if it were ambitious and wanted to be exalted with the threatening storm clouds. But never until tonight, never until now, have I gone through a tempest that drops fire! Either a civil war is going on in Heaven, or else the world, too saucy and insolent toward the gods, has incited them to send destruction upon it!"

"Why, have you seen you anything more wonderful than lightning and thunderbolts?" Cicero asked.

"I have seen a common slave — you know him well by sight — hold up his left hand, which did flame and burn like twenty torches joined together, and yet his hand, not feeling the fire, remained unburned. In addition — I have not since sheathed my sword — near the Capitol I met a surly lion that glared at me, and went by me without annoying me. Also, a hundred women looking like ghosts huddled together in a group because of their fear — they swore that they saw men all enclosed in fire walk up and down the streets. And yesterday the bird of night — the owl, a bird of bad omens — sat even at noonday in the marketplace, hooting and shrieking. When these prodigies occur all together, let men not say, 'These things have their reasons for occurring; they are natural.' I believe that they are omens of things to come."

"Indeed, it is a strange time," Cicero, who was unimpressed, said. "But men tend to interpret things however it suits them and they miss the things' true meaning."

He paused, and then asked, "Will Caesar go to the Capitol tomorrow?"

"He will," Casca replied. "He told Antony to send word to you that he will be there tomorrow."

"Good night then, Casca," Cicero said. "This disturbed and stormy sky is not good to walk in."

"Farewell, Cicero."

Cicero left, and Cassius walked up to Casca.

Cassius asked, "Who's there?"

"A Roman," Casca answered.

"Casca, by your voice."

"Your ear is good," Casca said. "Cassius, what a night is this!"

"It is a very pleasing night for honest men."

"Who ever knew that the Heavens could be so menacing?"

"Those who have realized that the Earth is full of faults," Cassius said. "For my part, I have walked about the streets, submitting myself to the perilous night, and, with my jacket open, Casca, as you see, I have bared my chest to the thunderbolt. And when the zigzag blue lightning seemed to open the breast of Heaven, I presented myself as a target just where the flashing thunderbolt was aimed."

"Why did you so much test the Heavens?" Casca asked. "It is the duty of men to fear and tremble when the mightiest gods send such dreadful signs and omens to terrify us."

"You are dull and stupid, Casca, and those sparks of life that should be in a Roman you do not have, or else you do not make use of them. You look pale and gaze and are afraid and throw yourself in a state of wonder to see the strange impatience of the Heavens, but if you would consider the true cause for why we see all these fires, why we see all these gliding ghosts, why we see birds and beasts depart from their usual natures, why we see old men, fools, and children make predictions and prophesy, why we see all these things change from their ordained behavior, their natures, and preformed faculties with which they were born and turn instead to unnatural behavior — why, you shall find that Heaven has infused them with these spirits and given them these powers to make them instruments of fear and warning about some unnatural state of affairs. I could, Casca, name to you a man who is very much like this dreadful night — this night that thunders, lightens, opens graves, and roars like the lion in the Capitol. He is a man no mightier than you or me in personal action, yet he has prodigiously grown and is as much to be afraid of as these strange events are."

"You mean Caesar, don't you, Cassius?" Casca asked.

"Let it be who it is. Romans today have the strong bodies of their ancestors, but unfortunately, we lack the minds of our fathers, and so the spirits of our mothers govern us instead. The yoke that has been placed on us and our endurance of this oppression show us to be like women."

"Indeed, the rumor is that the Senators tomorrow intend to establish Caesar as King," Casca said. "He shall wear his crown at sea and on land, in every place, except here in Italy."

"I know where I will wear this dagger then," Cassius said, displaying his dagger to Casca. "I will wear it in my heart. Cassius will deliver Cassius from bondage by committing suicide. By giving us the ability to commit suicide, you gods, you make the weak the strongest. By giving us the ability to commit suicide, you gods, you defeat tyrants. Neither stony tower, nor walls of beaten brass, nor airless dungeons, nor strong links of iron can confine a strong mind. But if a man grows weary of these worldly bars to freedom, he never lacks the power to kill himself. If I know this, then let everyone else in the world know it, too: That part of tyranny that affects me I can shake off whenever I want. Suicide is a way of escaping oppression."

Thunder sounded.

"I can also escape tyranny," Casca said. "So can every slave or prisoner. Each person's hand has the power to free that person from tyranny."

"But why should Caesar be a tyrant?" Cassius asked. "Poor man! I know he would prefer not to be a wolf, but he sees that the Romans are acting like sheep. He would be no lion if the Romans were not acting like hinds — female deer or peasants. People who want to quickly make a big fire start the fire with little pieces of straw. What trash is Rome, what rubbish and what offal are its citizens, when it serves as kindling to illuminate so vile a thing as Caesar! But what has my grief made me do? I may be speaking too freely to a person who is willing to be one of Caesar's slaves. In that case, news of what I have said will reach Caesar, and I will be punished. But I am armed, and I am indifferent to danger."

"You are speaking to Casca, and I am a man who is not a flattering tattletale. Shake my hand."

They shook hands, and Casca said, "If you are forming a faction against Caesar to set to rights all these wrongs, I will do as much as any of you."

"We have a deal," Cassius said. "Listen, Casca. I have already persuaded some of the noblest-minded Romans to undertake with me a dangerous enterprise whose outcome will be honorable. Right now, they are waiting for me at Pompey's porch — the colonnade outside Pompey's Theater. Because this night is filled with bad weather and things to be feared, no one is stirring or walking in the streets. This night is very bloody, fiery, and most terrible, just like the work we have in hand."

Seeing a man walking toward them, Casca said, "Hide because someone is walking quickly toward us."

Cassius looked and said, "It is Cinna. I recognize him by the way he walks. He is a friend."

Cassius then asked, "Cinna, where are you so quickly going?"

"To find you. Who's that? Metellus Cimber?"

Metellus Cimber's grievance against Julius Caesar was that Caesar had sent into exile Metellus Cimber's brother, Publius.

"No, it is Casca. He is now a part of our faction. Are the others waiting for me, Cinna?"

"I am glad that Casca is one of us," Cinna said. "What a fearful night this is! Two or three of us have seen strange sights tonight."

"Are the others waiting for me? Tell me that."

"Yes, they are waiting for you," Cinna replied. "Cassius, if only you could persuade the noble Brutus to join our faction —"

"Don't worry," Cassius said. "Good Cinna, take this letter and place it on the seat of the Praetor's chair. Brutus holds the office of Praetor, and he will find it. Throw this letter through his window. Use wax to affix this letter to the statue of Brutus' ancestor Lucius Junius Brutus. Once all of that is done, go to Pompey's porch, where you shall find us. Are Decius Brutus and Trebonius there?"

"Everyone is there except for Metellus Cimber. He left to seek you at your house. Well, I will hurry and do with these letters what you have asked me to do."

"Once you are done, meet us at the porch of Pompey's Theater."

Cinna departed, and Cassius said, "Come, Casca, you and I will before daybreak visit Brutus at his house. Three parts of him are ours already, and the next time we meet him, he will be entirely on our side."

"Brutus sits high in all the people's hearts — they respect him," Casca said. "If we act without him, we will be thought to be criminals, but if he acts with us, what we do will change, like alchemy changes lead to gold, to virtue and to worthiness."

"You understand Brutus and his worth and why we so greatly need him to be our side," Cassius said. "Let us go now because it is after midnight. Before day we will awaken him and make sure that he is on our side."

CHAPTER 2

— 2.1 —

Brutus was alone in his garden. He called for his young servant to come to him, "Lucius!"

He said to himself, "Tonight is stormy, so I cannot, by looking at the progress of the stars, tell how close to dawn it is."

Again he called, "Lucius, I say!"

He said to himself, "I wish that I were able to sleep as soundly as he does."

Again he called, "When are you coming, Lucius, when? Wake up, I say! Lucius!"

A sleepy Lucius went to Brutus and asked, "Did you call, my lord?"

"Get me a candle for my study, Lucius. When you have lit it, let me know."

"I will, my lord."

Lucius departed.

Brutus considered the reasons for assassinating Julius Caesar: "He will have to be killed. As for myself, I have no personal reason to kill him. I would kill him only for the general good. Caesar wants to be crowned as King. How that might change his nature, there's the question. Adders come out of hiding and sun themselves on a sunny day — and then you must be careful where you walk. Crown him as King? If we do that, we give him power — we give him a sting that he may use to hurt people at his discretion. Power is abused when the powerful lack compassion. To speak the truth about Caesar, I have never known him to be swayed by his emotions more than by his reason. But it is well known that people change after they acquire power. When a man starts to climb and acquire power, he starts low on the ladder. When he reaches the top of the ladder, he turns his back on those who are lower than himself. He looks at the clouds, scorning the base degrees by which he did ascend. Caesar may become like such men. To prevent that, we can kill him. We cannot justify killing him because of what he is now. We can justify killing him only because of what he may become later. Caesar, if he were given increased power, would begin to perform excesses of tyranny. We should think about Caesar the way we think about a serpent's egg. After the serpent is hatched, it will become

19

dangerous, as is its nature. Therefore, it is best to kill the serpent while it is still in the eggshell."

Lucius came back and said, "The candle is burning in your study, sir. Searching the window for a flint to light the candle with, I found this letter, thus sealed up. I am sure that it did not lie there when I went to bed."

Lucius handed Brutus the letter.

"Go back to bed. It is not yet day. Isn't tomorrow, boy, the Ides of March — March 15?"

"I don't know, sir."

"Look at the calendar, and tell me the date."

"I will, sir."

Lucius left to consult the calendar.

Brutus said to himself, "The meteors whizzing in the air give off so much light that I may read by them."

He opened the letter and read out loud, "Brutus, you are sleeping. Wake up and see yourself. Shall Rome, et cetera. Speak, strike, and correct political abuses!"

He repeated some words from the letter: "Brutus, you are sleeping. Wake up!"

He said, "Such calls to action have been often dropped where I have picked them up. I must try to understand what is meant by 'Shall Rome, et cetera.' I need to fill in the gaps. Shall Rome submit to the power of one man? What, Rome? My ancestors did from the streets of Rome drive the last King of Rome out. 'Speak, strike, and correct political abuses!' Am I being entreated to speak and to strike? Rome, I make you a promise: If the correction of political wrongs will follow the speaking and the striking, Brutus will do everything that is asked of him here."

Lucius came back and said, "Sir, tomorrow is the Ides of March."

Brutus said, "Good."

Knocks sounded on the gate.

Brutus said, "Go to the gate; somebody is knocking."

Lucius left to go to the gate and see who was knocking.

Brutus said to himself, "Since Cassius first did incite me to oppose Caesar, I have not slept. Between the acting of a dreadful thing and the first thought of doing it, the entire interim is like a hallucination or a hideous dream. The person is conflicted and debates within himself, and he is like a little Kingdom that suffers from civil war."

Lucius came back and said, "Sir, your brother-in-law Cassius is at the gate, and he wants to see you."

"Is he alone?"

"No, sir. Some men are with him."

"Do you know them?"

"No, sir. Their hats are pulled down about their ears, and half of each man's face is buried in his cloak, and so I was not able to recognize any of the men."

"Let them in."

Lucius left to let the men in to see Brutus.

Brutus said to himself, "They are the faction of conspirators. Conspiracy, are you ashamed to show your dangerous brow by night, when evils are most common and free to roam about? By day, where will you find a cavern dark enough to hide your monstrous face? You need not seek a cave, conspiracy. You can hide your monstrous faces behind smiles and friendliness. If you were to go on your way with your monstrous face revealed, not even the darkness of Erebus, a part of the Underworld, could hide you enough to keep your plot from being detected and stopped."

The conspirators entered the garden: Cassius, Casca, Decius Brutus, Cinna, Metellus Cimber, and Trebonius.

Cassius said, "I am afraid that we have come too early and disturbed your rest. Good morning, Brutus. Do we trouble you?"

"I have been up for an hour; I have been awake all night," Brutus said. "Do I know these men who have come along with you?"

"Yes, you know all of them," Cassius said. "Every man here respects you, and everyone wishes that you had that opinion of yourself that every noble Roman has of you."

Cassius began to name the men who had come with him: "This is Trebonius."

"He is welcome here," Brutus said.

"This is Decius Brutus."

"He is welcome, too."

"This is Casca, this is Cinna, and this is Metellus Cimber."

"They are all welcome," Brutus said. "What cares have kept you awake all night?"

Cassius replied, "Can I speak to you privately?"

Cassius and Brutus moved away a little and whispered to each other.

Decius Brutus said to the conspirators with him, "This way lies the East. Isn't this the point where the Sun rises?"

"No," Casca said.

"Pardon me," Cinna said, "but the Sun does rise there. The gray lines that streak the clouds show that the Sun is rising there."

"You shall confess that you are both deceived," Casca said. "Here, where I am pointing my sword, the Sun rises. It is further to the South because we are still so early in the year. Two months from now, the Sun will rise at a point further North. Due East is here, where the Capitol stands."

An impartial observer might think that if the conspirators did not even know where the Sun rose that this might be an ominous omen of their future.

Brutus and Cassius had finished their private conversation.

Brutus said to the conspirators, "Let me shake your hands, each of you."

"And let us swear our commitment," Cassius said.

"No, let us not swear an oath," Brutus said. "We do not need to. We have the sad looks on citizens' faces, the suffering of our own souls, and the evil abuses of our times. If these are weak motives for what we are planning to do, then let us stop now and every man go home to his bed of idleness. If these are weak motives for what we are planning to do, then let the tyranny that looks down on us from a great height continue its reign until each man of us drops like men chosen to be punished at a tyrant's whim. But if we have good motives, as I am sure that we do, motives that bear enough fire to kindle cowards and to steel with valor the melting spirits of women, then, countrymen, what else do we need to spur us to action? We have good motives that lead us to correct the errors of our times. What other bond do we need than that of Romans who are capable of keeping secrets and have given their word and will not back down from what they have said that they will do? What other oath do we need than that of one honest man to another that we will do what we promised to do or die while trying to do it? Let priests swear and cowards and men who are overly cautious and old and feeble carcass-like men and such suffering souls as welcome wrongs. Let untrustworthy men swear oaths for bad causes. We ought not to stain the impartial virtue of our enterprise or our indomitable will with the belief that either our cause or our actions require an oath. All of us know that every drop of blood that a noble Roman has would be guilty of an act of baseness if the Roman would break the smallest particle of any promise that he had made.”

“What about Cicero?” Cassius said. “Shall we talk to him and see if he wants to join our conspiracy? I think he will stand very strong with us.”

“Let us not leave Cicero out,” Casca said.

“No, by no means,” Cinna said.

“Let us have him as a member of our conspiracy,” Metellus Cimber said, “for his silver hairs will buy for us a good reputation and persuade people to commend our deeds. People will say that he came up with the conspiracy and we followed his lead. Our youth and wildness shall in no way be mentioned; people will instead talk about Cicero’s maturity.”

“Don’t mention Cicero,” Brutus said. “Let us not tell him about our plot because he will never follow anything that other men begin.”

Brutus had much influence with the other conspirators.

“Then we will leave him out of our conspiracy,” Cassius said.

“Indeed, he is not fit to be in our conspiracy,” Casca said.

“Shall only Caesar be killed?” Decius Brutus asked.

“Decius, that is an important question,” Cassius said. “I don’t think it is wise to allow Mark Antony, who is so well beloved by Caesar, to outlive Caesar. We shall find that Antony is a dangerous plotter. He has resources, and if he adds to them, they may be great enough to hurt all of us. To prevent Antony from becoming a great enemy to us, we should kill both Caesar and Antony.”

“If we do that, our actions will seem too bloody, Caius Cassius,” Brutus said. “To cut the head off and then hack the limbs will make it seem like we killed at first with anger and subsequently killed with envy. Antony is but a limb of Caesar. Let us be sacrificers, but not butchers, Caius. We all stand up against the spirit of Caesar. His spirit is tyrannous. In the spirit of men there is no blood, and I wish that we could kill Caesar’s spirit without dismembering Caesar’s body! Unfortunately, Caesar’s body must bleed! Gentle friends, let us kill Caesar’s body boldly, but not wrathfully. When we kill, it ought to be like we are making a sacrifice to the gods, not like we are butchering an animal and throwing pieces of meat to the dogs. Let’s carve Caesar as a sacrificial dish fit for the gods, not hew him as a carcass fit for hounds. And let our hearts, our subtle masters, stir up our limbs to an act of rage, and afterward be seen to chide them. This shall make our purpose appear to be necessary — and not envious. If the commoners understand that, we shall be called purgers of an evil, not murderers of a man. As for Mark Antony, let us not worry about him because he can do no more than Caesar's arm can do after Caesar's head is cut off."

"Still, I fear him," Cassius said. "For in the deeply rooted love that Antony bears to Caesar —"

"Good Cassius, do not worry about Antony," Brutus said. "If he loves Caesar, all that he can do is what he can do to himself. He can mourn Caesar and commit suicide. Even that is too much to ask him to do because he spends his time enjoying entertainments, wild pleasures, and too much company."

"We need not fear Antony," Trebonius said, "so we need not kill him. Let Antony live, and later he will laugh at what we do."

A clock struck.

"Quiet!" Brutus said. "Count the number of times the clock strikes."

They listened.

"The clock struck three times," Cassius said.

"It is time to go," Trebonius said.

"It is not certain whether Caesar will go to the Capitol today or not," Cassius said, "because he has grown superstitious lately. His opinion now is much different from what he formerly and strongly believed about visions, dreams, and omens. It may be the case that these apparent omens of disaster, the unusual terror of this night, and the persuasion of his fortune tellers may keep him from going to the Capitol today."

"Don't worry about that," Decius Brutus said. "If he decides not to go to the Capitol, I can persuade him to go. He loves to hear about tales of traps — how unicorns can be trapped by charging at a man who moves aside and lets the unicorn's horn deeply penetrate a tree, how bears can be trapped by being fascinated with a mirror, how elephants can be trapped when they fall into holes, how lions can be trapped in nets, and how men can be trapped by flatterers. But when I tell Caesar that he hates flatterers, he agrees with me, and he is then most flattered. Let me work on him. I can persuade him to act the way we want him to act, and I will bring him with me to the Capitol."

"No, not you alone," Cassius said. "All of us will be there to bring him to the Capitol."

"By eight o'clock?" Brutus asked. "Is that the hour we decided on?"

"That is the hour," Cinna said. "Do not fail to be there by then."

"Caius Ligarius bears a grudge against Caesar because Caesar berated him for speaking well of Pompey," Metellus Cimber said. "I am surprised that none of you has thought of inviting him to join our conspiracy."

"Metellus Cimber, go and visit him," Brutus said. "He respects me, and I have done favors for him. Send him to visit me, and I will persuade him to join our conspiracy."

"Morning is coming," Cassius said. "We will leave now, Brutus. Friends, scatter yourselves; do not walk in a group. Everyone, remember what you have promised to do, and show yourselves true Romans."

"Good gentlemen, look fresh and merry," Brutus said. "Don't let your faces reveal our plot. Instead, act as our Roman actors act. Act with unflagging spirits and your usual dignified behavior. Good night to each of you."

The conspirators departed, leaving Brutus alone in his garden.

Brutus called, "Boy! Lucius! Fast asleep? It does not matter. Enjoy the honey-heavy dew of slumber. You have no problems or fantasies of the imagination that worry the brains of men under stress and therefore you are able to sleep so soundly."

Portia, Brutus' wife, now walked up to him.

"Brutus, my lord!"

"Portia, is something wrong? Why are you up now? It is not good for your health to expose yourself to the raw and cold morning."

"It is not good for your health, either," Portia said. "You are acting strangely and ignoring me. You abruptly got out of our bed, Brutus, and yesterday, at supper, you suddenly arose, and walked about, musing and sighing, with your arms folded across your chest, and when I asked you what the matter was, you stared at me rudely. I asked you again, and then you scratched your head and very impatiently stamped your foot. Again I asked you, yet you would not answer my question. Instead, with an angry wave of your hand, you gave me a sign to leave you, and so I did. I was afraid to strengthen your impatience and anger that already seemed too much enflamed, and I hoped that you were simply in a bad mood, which sometimes happens to every man. But your bad mood will not let you eat, talk, or sleep. If your bad mood could change your face and body as much as it has changed your personality, I would not be able to recognize you, Brutus. My dear husband, tell me what is bothering you.”

“I am ill. That is all,” Brutus said.

“Brutus, you are wise, and if you were suffering from ill health, you would do something to restore yourself to good health.”

“Why, so I do,” Brutus said. “Good Portia, go to bed.”

“Is my Brutus sick? Is it healthy to walk around uncovered and breathe the unhealthy vapors of a dank morning? What, is my Brutus sick, and therefore he steals out of his wholesome bed to dare the vile contagion of the night and give the diseased and unpurified-by-the-Sun air a chance to add to his sickness? No, my Brutus. You do not normally act like that. You have some sickness inside your mind, which, by the right and virtue of my position as your wife, I ought to know about.”

Portia knelt before her husband and said, “Upon my knees, I urge you, by my once-commended beauty, by all your vows of love and that great vow that married us and made us one, that you tell me, who is yourself and your half, why you are burdened by trouble. I also urge you to tell me about the men tonight who came to talk to you — the some six or seven men who kept their faces hidden even from darkness.”

“Do not kneel before me, gentle Portia,” Brutus said.

“I would have no reason to kneel before you,” Portia, still kneeling, said, “if you still acted like the gentle Brutus whom I married. Tell me, Brutus, why aren’t you telling me your secrets? Shouldn’t a wife know them, or is there some exception to a marriage contract? Am I made one with you only partially — only when it comes to eating meals with you, to be a comfort to you in bed and sleep with you, and to talk to you sometimes? Do I dwell only in the suburbs of your good pleasure? The Roman suburbs are where the whorehouses are, and if I dwell only in the suburbs of your good pleasure, then I, Portia, am only Brutus’ harlot and not his wife.”

“You are my true and honorable wife, and you are as dear to me as are the ruddy drops of blood that visit my sad heart.”

“If what you are saying is true, then I ought to know your secrets. I grant I am a woman; but I am a woman whom Lord Brutus took to be his wife. I grant I am a woman, but I am a woman who is well reputed — I am the daughter of

Marcus Porcius Cato, who fought for Pompey in the civil war and who chose to commit suicide rather than be captured by Julius Caesar. Can you think that I am no stronger than other women when I have such a father and such a husband? Tell me your secrets; I will not reveal them. I have done something to prove my trustworthiness — I have given myself a voluntary wound here in my thigh. Can I bear that pain with patience, and yet not be able to keep my husband's secrets?"

"Oh, you gods, make me worthy of this noble wife!"

Knocks sounded on the gate.

Brutus said, "Listen! Someone is knocking! Portia, go inside for a while. Soon, I will tell you the secrets of my heart. Everything that I have promised to do I will tell you. I will tell you everything that has been affecting the way I look and act. For now, quickly leave me."

Portia exited.

Brutus asked, "Lucius, who was knocking?"

Lucius and Caius Ligarius, who held a handkerchief against his nose and mouth, walked up to Brutus.

Lucius said, "Here is a sick man who would speak with you."

Brutus said, "He is Caius Ligarius, whom Metellus Cimber spoke about."

He told Lucius, "Boy, go back inside."

Then he said, "Caius Ligarius! How are you?"

"Please accept my 'good morning' from my feeble and ill tongue," he replied.

"What a time have you chosen to be ill, brave Caius, and use a handkerchief as a protection against drafts!" Brutus said. "I wish that you were not sick!"

"I am not sick, if Brutus has in mind an exploit that is worthy of the name of honor."

"Such an exploit have I in mind, Ligarius, if you have a healthy ear to hear it."

"By all the gods that Romans bow before, I here discard my sickness!" Ligarius said. "Soul of Rome! Brave son, derived from honorable loins! You, like an exorcist, have raised my deadened spirit. Tell me what to do, and I will try to do impossible things — and I will do them, too. What needs to be done?"

"A piece of work that will make sick men whole."

"But are not some men whole whom we must make sick?"

"That must we also do," Brutus said. "What must be done, Caius Ligarius, I shall tell you as we are walking to the person to whom it must be done."

"Start walking," Ligarius said, "and with a heart newly fired, I will follow you. I don't know yet what needs to be done, but I am happy nevertheless because it is Brutus who is leading me."

"Follow me, then," Brutus said.

— 2.2 —

Julius Caesar was alone in a room in his house. Outside, the storm continued to thunder and lightning.

Caesar said to himself, "Neither Heaven nor Earth has been at peace tonight. Three times my wife, Calpurnia, has in her sleep cried out, 'Help! They are murdering Caesar!'"

He heard a noise and asked, "Who is there?"

A servant entered the room and said, "My lord?"

Caesar ordered, "Go and tell the priests to perform a sacrifice immediately. After they are done, return and tell me what they have learned from the sacrifice."

"I will, my lord."

The servant departed, and Calpurnia entered the room.

She said to her husband, "What do you mean to do today, Caesar? Are you thinking of going to the Capitol? Today, you will not leave this house."

"Caesar shall go forth today. The things that have threatened me have never looked anywhere but at my back. Whenever they see the face of Caesar, they vanish."

"Caesar, I have never paid attention to omens, yet now they frighten me. Someone in our house — besides the things that we have heard and seen — has told me the most horrid sights that the watchman has seen. A lioness has given birth in the streets. Graves have yawned and yielded up their dead. Fierce fiery warriors have fought upon the clouds in ranks and squadrons and square formations — these soldiers drizzled blood upon the Capitol, and the noise of battle hurtled in the air. Horses neighed, and dying men groaned, and ghosts shrieked and squealed in the streets. Caesar! These things are unnatural, and I fear them."

"How it is possible to avoid something that the mighty gods have decreed? Today Caesar shall go forth. These predictions and omens apply to the world in general as well as to Caesar."

"When beggars die, no comets are seen. The Heavens themselves blaze to announce the death of princes," Calpurnia replied.

"Cowards die many times before their deaths; the valiant never taste of death but once. Of all the wonders that I yet have heard, it seems to me the very strangest that men should fear death because death, a necessary end, will come when it will come."

The servant returned, and Caesar asked him, "What do the augurers — the tellers of futures — say?"

"They would not have you go out of the house today," the servant said. "Plucking the entrails of a sacrificial offering, they could not find a heart within the beast."

"The gods do this to shame cowards — they dislike cowards," Caesar said. "Caesar would be a beast without a heart, if he would stay at home today for fear. No, Caesar shall not stay home. Danger knows full well that Caesar is more dangerous than he is. We are two lions that littered in the same day. I am the elder and more terrible of us two, and Caesar shall go forth today."

"Your wisdom is eaten up by overconfidence," Calpurnia said. "Do not go forth today. Say that it is my fear that keeps you in the house, and you yourself are not afraid. We will send Mark Antony to the Senate, and he shall say that you are not well today."

She knelt and said, "Let me, upon my knee, prevail in this. Do what I want you to do. Stay at home today."

Caesar raised her to her feet and said, "Mark Antony shall say that I am not well, and, because you want me to, I will stay at home."

Decius Brutus entered the room.

Caesar said, "Here's Decius Brutus — he shall tell the Senators the news."

"Caesar, all hail!" Decius Brutus said. "Good morning, worthy Caesar. I have come to walk with you to the Senate House."

"You have come at a good time," Caesar said. "You can carry my greeting to the Senators and tell them that I will not come today. To say that I cannot come is false, and to say that I dare not come is falser. I will not come today. Tell the Senators that, Decius."

"Say that he is sick," Calpurnia said.

Julius Caesar immediately decided not to have this said about him, although he had just told Calpurnia that Mark Antony would tell the Senators that he — Caesar — was not well. He disliked appearing weak.

"Shall Caesar send a lie?" Julius Caesar said. "I have made extensive conquests in war — should I be afraid to tell gray-bearded Senators the truth? Decius, go tell them that Caesar will not come."

"Most mighty Caesar, let me know the reason why you are not coming, lest I be laughed at when I tell them that you are not coming."

"The cause is in my will: I will not come," Caesar said. "That is enough to satisfy the Senators. But for your private satisfaction, because I respect you, I will let you know my reason. Calpurnia here, my wife, wants me to stay at home. She dreamt this night that she saw my statue, like a fountain with a hundred spouts, running with pure blood. Many vigorous Romans came smiling, and bathed their hands in the blood. This she interprets as a warning and a portent. She believes that evils are imminent, and on her knee she has begged me to stay at home today."

"This dream has been misinterpreted," Decius Brutus said. "The vision is fair and fortunate — it foretells good fortune. Your statue spouting blood through many holes, blood in which so many smiling Romans bathed, signifies that from you great Rome shall suck reviving blood, and that great men shall strive to get honors from you and souvenirs to venerate, and that they will be your servants. This is the true meaning of Calpurnia's dream."

"You have well interpreted the dream," Caesar said.

"Yes, I have, as you shall know when you have heard what I have to tell you now," Decius Brutus said. "The Senators have decided to give this day a crown to mighty Caesar. If you send them word that you will not come to the Senate today, they may change their minds. Besides, if you do not come to the Senate today, someone is likely to joke, 'We should adjourn the Senate until after Caesar's wife has had better dreams.' If Caesar stays at home, won't the Senators and people whisper, 'Caesar is afraid'? Pardon me, Caesar, but my high hopes for your advancement make me tell you this, and my respect for you has outweighed my manners."

"How foolish do your fears seem now, Calpurnia!" Caesar said. "I am ashamed I yielded to them. Give me my cloak, for I will go."

Publius, an old Senator, entered the room.

Caesar said, "Look, Publius has come to fetch me."

"Good morning, Caesar," Publius said.

"Welcome, Publius," Caesar said.

Brutus, Ligarius, Metellus, Casca, Trebonius, and Cinna entered the room.

"What, Brutus, are you up so early, too?" Caesar said, adding, "Good morning, Casca."

Caesar then said, "Caius Ligarius, Caesar was never so much your enemy as that illness that has made you lean."

Ligarius had supported Pompey in the civil war, but Caesar had pardoned him.

Caesar asked, "What time is it?"

"Caesar, the clock has struck eight o'clock," Brutus answered.

"I thank you for your trouble and courtesy in coming here to accompany me to the Senate House," Caesar said.

Mark Antony entered the room.

"Look! Even Antony, who revels long into the nights, is up," Caesar said. "Good morning to you, Antony."

"And to you, most noble Caesar," Antony replied.

Caesar ordered a servant, "Set out some wine."

He said to his guests, "I am to blame for making you wait. Cinna, Metellus, and Trebonius, I want to talk with you for an hour today. Remember to talk to me later today. Stay near me so that I will remember."

"Caesar, I will," Trebonius said. He thought, *I will be so near to you that your best friends shall wish I had been further away.*

"Good friends, let us go in this other room, and you can drink some wine with me, and then we, like the friends we are, will leave together."

Brutus thought, *We are now only like friends — we are not really friends. Caesar, this makes my heart ache.*

— 2.3 —

On a Roman street on which Caesar would soon walk, Artemidorus read a letter that he had written:

"Caesar, beware of Brutus; take heed of Cassius; do not go near Casca; keep an eye on Cinna; do not trust Trebonius; pay attention to Metellus Cimber; Decius Brutus does not like you; you have wronged Caius Ligarius. All of these men are of the same mind, and that mind is opposed to Caesar. Unless you are immortal, watch out for yourself. Your overconfidence gives conspiracy an opportunity. May the mighty gods defend you! Your good friend, Artemidorus."

Artemidorus said to himself, "I will wait here until Caesar passes by, and I will give him this letter as if it were a petition — a request that a wrong be righted. My heart laments that good men cannot live safely out of the way of the teeth of jealous rivals. If you read this, Caesar, you may live. If you do not read this, the Fates are on the side of traitors."

— 2.4 —

On a Roman street, Portia ordered Lucius, "Boy, run to the Senate House. Do not stay — go now! Why are you still here?"

"I need to know what errand you want me to do, madam," Lucius said.

"If I could, I would have had you there and back again before I could tell you what you should do there," Portia said.

She said to herself, "Firmness of mind, come to me and support me! Set a huge mountain — a barrier — in between my heart and my tongue! I have a man's mind, but a woman's might. How hard it is for women to keep secrets!"

She said to Lucius, "Are you still here?"

"Madam, what do you want to do? Run to the Capitol, and nothing else? And then return to you, and nothing else?"

"Yes, run there and back, boy. Tell me if Brutus looks well. When he left here, he looked ill. Also, see what Caesar is doing. See which petitioners crowd against him."

She thought that she heard a noise and said, "Listen, boy! What is that noise?"

"I don't hear anything, madam."

"Please, listen carefully. I heard a sound like a fight or a battle, and the wind brought it from the Capitol."

"Madam, I hear nothing."

The soothsayer walked up to Portia and Lucius.

Portia said to him, "Come here, fellow. From which way have you come?"

"I have come from my own house, good lady," the soothsayer replied.

"What time is it?"

"About nine o'clock, lady."

"Has Caesar gone to the Capitol?"

"Madam, not yet. I am going to find a spot to stand to see him pass on his way to the Capitol."

"You have some request to make to Caesar, haven't you?"

"That I have, lady," the soothsayer replied. "If it will please Caesar to be so good to Caesar as to hear me, I shall beg him to befriend himself."

"Why, do you know of any harm that is intended towards him?"

"None that I know will happen, but much that I fear may happen," the soothsayer replied. "Good morning to you. I must go. Here the street is narrow, and the throng of people who follow Caesar at the heels — Senators, Praetors, common people — will crowd a feeble man almost to death. I'll go to a place with more room, and there I will speak to great Caesar as he comes along."

Portia said, "I must go inside. How weak a thing is the heart of a woman! Brutus, may the Heavens help you in your enterprise!"

She had said that aloud. Afraid, she thought, *The boy Lucius must have heard me.*

She said out loud so that Lucius would hear her, "Brutus has a petition that Caesar will not grant."

She added, "I am growing faint. Run, Lucius, and commend me to my lord. Say that I am cheerful, then return to me and tell me what he says to you."

CHAPTER 3

In front of the Capitol, Julius Caesar and many others were standing. Among them were Artemidorus and the soothsayer, Brutus, Cassius, Casca, Decius Brutus, Metellus Cimber, Trebonius, Cinna, Mark Antony, Lepidus, Popilius Lena, Publius, and others.

Caesar said to the soothsayer, "The Ides of March have come."

"Yes, Caesar, but they have not yet gone," the soothsayer replied.

"Hail, Caesar!" Artemidorus said. "Read my petition."

Eager to deflect Caesar's attention away from Artemidorus, Decius Brutus, one of the conspirators, said to Caesar, "Trebonius asks you to read this humble petition at your leisure."

"Caesar, read my petition first," Artemidorus said. "My petition concerns you personally. Read it, great Caesar."

"What concerns myself, I will read last," Caesar said.

"Please do not wait," Artemidorus said. "Read it now."

"What! Is the fellow insane?" Caesar said.

Publius said to Artemidorus, "Fellow, get out of the way."

Cassius said to Artemidorus, "Why are you urging Caesar to read your petition in the street? Go to the Capitol with your petition."

Caesar and several other people went to the Senate House.

Popilius Lena, a Roman Senator, said to Cassius, who had stayed behind, "I hope that your enterprise today thrives."

"What enterprise, Popilius?"

"Fare you well," Popilius Lena said and then followed Caesar.

Brutus asked Cassius, "What did Popilius Lena say to you?"

"He said that he hopes our enterprise may thrive. I fear that our plot has been discovered."

"Popilius is going up to Caesar," Brutus said. "Let's see what happens."

Cassius said, "Casca, be quick of action. We fear that our plot has been revealed."

He said to Brutus, "What shall we do? If our plot is known, either Cassius or Caesar will die. If we fail to kill Caesar, I will kill myself."

"Cassius, be steady. Popilius Lena is not telling Caesar about our plot. Look, be steady and resolute," Brutus replied. "Popilius is smiling, and Caesar's expression has not changed."

Cassius said, "Trebonius knows the right time to play his part in this plot. Look, Brutus, he is drawing Mark Antony out of the way."

Trebonius and Mark Antony left.

Decius Brutus asked, "Where is Metellus Cimber? He needs to go and immediately make his petition to Caesar."

"He is ready," Brutus said. "Crowd near Metellus Cimber and second his petition."

Cinna said, "Casca, you will be the first to raise your hand and stab Caesar."

"Are we all ready?" Caesar asked. "What is now amiss that Caesar and his Senate must set to rights?"

Metellus Cimber said, "Most high, most mighty, and most powerful Caesar, Metellus Cimber kneels before you with a humble heart —"

He knelt, but Caesar said, "I must stop you, Metellus Cimber. This stooping and bowing might thrill the blood of ordinary men and influence them to turn aside ancient customs and laws and change them like the whims of children making up rules for a game. Do not be so foolish as to think that Caesar's spirit can rebel against its true nature because of these things that influence fools. I refer to sweet words, knee-bending bows, and cringing like a cocker spaniel. Your brother, Publius Cimber, has been banished from Rome by my decree. If you bow and pray and fawn for him, I will kick you out of my way as if you were a cur. Know that Caesar is not doing the wrong thing by keeping your brother in exile, and without good cause and reasons he will not be convinced to allow your brother to return from exile."

Metellus Cimber replied, "Is there no voice more worthy than my own to speak more sweetly in great Caesar's ear and urge the return of my banished brother?"

Brutus knelt and kissed Caesar's hand and said, "I kiss your hand, but not in flattery, Caesar. I urge that Publius Cimber may immediately be recalled from exile."

An impartial observer could think that Brutus was kissing Caesar's hand in betrayal.

"What are you saying, Brutus!" Caesar said.

"Grant your pardon, Caesar," Cassius said, falling to Caesar's feet. "Caesar, grant your pardon. I, Cassius, fall to your feet and beg that Publius Cimber be allowed to return to Rome and to have all Roman rights restored to him."

"If I were like you, I could be persuaded to change my mind," Caesar said. "But I am as constant as the Northern star, the pole star that sailors use to navigate their ships. The Northern star's fixed and permanent position has no equal in the Heavens. The skies are painted with innumerable sparks of stars. They are all fire and each of them shines, but of all the stars only one continually keeps his position. It is the same with people in the world. Many men live on Earth, and men are flesh and blood, and capable of understanding, yet in all the numbers of men I know of only one who — unassailable — keeps the same position, undisturbed by the motion of other men, and that man is me. Let me demonstrate this, here and now. I banished Publius Cimber, and I continue to banish him."

Cinna said, "Caesar —"

Caesar said, "Stop! Would you try to lift Mount Olympus, the abode of the gods?"

Decius Brutus said, "Great Caesar —"

Caesar said, "Why are you pleading with me when even my good friend Brutus is kneeling before me and not swaying me?"

Casca said, "Speak, hands, for me!"

Casca would not speak with words, but with his sword.

Casca stabbed Caesar first, and then all of the other conspirators stabbed Caesar.

When Brutus stabbed Julius Caesar, Caesar looked him directly in the eyes and said, "*Et tu, Brute!* You, too, Brutus? Then let Caesar fall and die!"

He fell before a statue of Pompey.

Over Caesar's dead body, Cinna shouted, "Liberty! Freedom! Tyranny is dead! Run around, proclaim Caesar's death, cry it about the streets."

Brutus said to the non-conspirators present, "People and Senators, do not be frightened. Don't run away. Stay here. Ambition's debt is paid. Caesar was ambitious, and he has died for it."

"Go to the speakers' platform, Brutus, and speak," Casca said.

Decius Brutus said, "Cassius should also speak from one of the speakers' platforms."

"Where is old Publius?" Brutus asked.

"He is here, stunned by this mutiny," Cinna said.

"Let us stand close together in case some friend of Caesar's should happen —" Metellus Cimber began to say.

"We have no need of defending ourselves," Brutus interrupted.

He added, "Publius, be of good cheer — don't worry. We mean you no harm. We will not hurt you or any other Roman. Tell the other Romans that, Publius."

"And leave us now, Publius," Cassius said, "lest the people, rushing here, should hurt an elderly man such as you."

"Do as Cassius tells you, Publius," Brutus said. "No one should suffer from the consequences of this deed except we who committed it."

Trebonius walked up to the conspirators.

"Where is Mark Antony?" Cassius asked.

"He has fled to his house, stupefied," Trebonius replied. "Men, wives, and children stare, cry out, and run in the streets as if it were Doomsday — the Day of Judgment."

"Fates, we will know your pleasures — we will know what you have in store for us," Brutus said. "That we shall die, we know, but men are concerned about the time of their death and how to prolong their lives."

"Why, he who cuts off twenty years of life cuts off so many years of fearing death," Cassius said.

"If that is true, then death is a benefit," Brutus said. "We are Caesar's friends because we have shortened the time that he will fear death. Stoop, Romans, stoop, and let us bathe our hands in Caesar's blood up to the elbows and smear our swords with his blood. Then we will walk forth, all the way to the Forum, and, waving our red and bloody weapons over our heads, let us all cry, 'Peace, freedom, and liberty!'"

"Stoop, then, and wash your hands in Caesar's blood," Cassius said.

The conspirators bloodied their hands and swords with Caesar's blood.

"For many ages hereafter, this our lofty scene will be acted in celebration in countries that do not yet exist and with languages not yet known!" Cassius said.

Brutus said, "How many times shall Caesar bleed again in plays, although he now lies — worthless as dust — at the base of this statue of Pompey!"

"As often as the plays are given," Cassius said, "that often shall we conspirators be called the men who gave their country liberty!"

An impartial observer who knew future history would think that no, the conspirators' attempt to keep Rome a republic would fail. Octavius Caesar would become Caesar Augustus, the first Roman Emperor. Now, he is better known as Caesar Augustus than as Octavius.

"Shall we leave now?" Decius Brutus asked.

"Yes," Cassius said. "Let all of us go now. Brutus shall lead, and we will follow his heels with the very boldest and best hearts of Rome."

A servant came toward the group of conspirators.

Brutus said, "Wait! Who is coming here? It is a friend of Mark Antony's."

The servant knelt and said, "Brutus, thus did my master order me to kneel before you. Thus Mark Antony ordered me to fall down; and, with me kneeling before you, he ordered me to say this to you: 'Brutus is noble, wise, valiant, and honorable. Caesar was mighty, bold, royal, and loving. Say that I feared Caesar, honored him, and loved him. If Brutus will swear that Antony may safely come to him, and be convinced that Caesar deserved to die, then Mark Antony shall not love the dead Caesar as well as he loves the living Brutus. With all true faith, he will follow the fortunes and affairs of noble Brutus through the hazards of this unfamiliar state of affairs.' So says my master Antony."

"Your master is a wise and valiant Roman," Brutus said. "I have never thought any less of him. Tell him that if it will please him to come here, we will explain everything to his satisfaction. I swear that he will depart from us untouched and unharmed."

"I will bring him here immediately," the servant said, and then exited.

"I know that Mark Antony will be a good friend to us," Brutus said.

"I hope that he will," Cassius said, "but yet I greatly fear him. My suspicions always are accurate."

"Here comes Antony," Brutus said.

Mark Antony went to the group of conspirators.

Brutus said, "Welcome, Mark Antony."

Looking at Caesar's bloody corpse, Mark Antony said, "Oh, mighty Caesar! Do you lie so low? Are all your conquests, glories, triumphs, and spoils shrunk to this little measure of ground that your body lies on? Farewell."

Mark Antony then said to the conspirators, "I do not know, gentlemen, what you intend, who else must bleed and die, who else you consider to be rank. If you intend to kill me, this is the hour to kill me and these are the weapons to use to kill me: There is no hour as fit as the hour of Caesar's death, nor no instruments of death half as worthy as your swords, made rich with the most noble blood of all this world. I do beg of you, if you have a grudge against me, now, while your reddened hands do reek and smoke with hot blood, to kill me and feel your pleasure. Even if I were to live a thousand years, I shall not find myself as ready to die as I am now. No place to die will please me as much as this place, no way to die will please me as much as here by Caesar to be cut down by you — the choice and master spirits of this age."

"Antony, do not beg us to kill you," Brutus said. "Though now we must appear bloody and cruel, as, by the blood on our hands and by the blood on the corpse of Caesar you see we do, yet all you can see is only our hands and this bleeding business they have done. You cannot see our hearts, which are full of pity for Caesar and full of a greater pity for the wrongs that Caesar committed against Rome. As fire drives out fire, so pity drives out pity. Our greater pity drove out our lesser pity, and we killed Caesar. As for you, do not be afraid — for you, Mark Antony, our swords are blunted. Our arms, which have the power to harm, and our hearts, which are filled with brotherly love, embrace you with kind love, good thoughts, and respect."

"Your voice and your opinion shall be as strong as any man's when it comes to deciding how to distribute new political offices and awards," Cassius said.

"Be patient until we have appeased and soothed the multitude of people, who are beside themselves with fear, and then we will explain to you the reasons why I, who loved Caesar when I struck him, have killed him," Brutus said.

"I do not doubt your wisdom," Mark Antony said.

He proceeded to shake the conspirators' hands, saying, "Let each man give me his bloody hand to shake. First, Marcus Brutus, I will shake hands with you. Next, Caius Cassius, do I take your hand and shake it. Now, Decius Brutus, yours. Now yours, Metellus. Yours, Cinna; and, my valiant Casca, yours. Though I shake your hand last, you are not last in my respect, good Trebonius."

He added, "Gentlemen — what shall I say? My reputation now stands on such slippery ground that you must consider me in one of two bad ways. You must consider me to be either a coward or a flatterer."

He looked at the corpse of Caesar and said, "That I did love you, Caesar, is true. If your spirit looks upon us now, shall it not grieve you more than your death, to see your Antony making his peace, shaking the bloody fingers of your foes — your most noble foes — in the presence of your corpse? Had I as many eyes as you have wounds, weeping as fast as your wounds stream forth your blood, it would become me better than to close in terms of friendship with your enemies. It is much better that I cry than shake hands with your enemies. Pardon me, Julius! Here you were hunted down like a deer, brave heart. Here you fell, and here your hunters stand, marked by your slaughter and reddened by your life stream of blood. The world was the forest of this deer, and you were the dear of this world. The world was Caesar's territory, and Caesar was the life stream of the world. How like a deer, struck by many princes, do you lie here!"

"Mark Antony —" Cassius began to say.

"Pardon me, Caius Cassius," Mark Antony said, "Even the enemies of Caesar shall say what I just said. So then, when a friend of Caesar says it, it is a cool and moderate assessment."

"I do not blame you for praising Caesar in that way," Cassius said, "but what agreement do you mean to have with us? Will you be one of our friends, or shall we proceed and not depend on you?"

"I shook your hands in friendship just now, but I was, indeed, distracted when I looked down at the corpse of Caesar. I am friends with you all and I respect you all, with the hope that you shall give me reasons why and in what way was Caesar dangerous."

"If we cannot do that, then this corpse here would be a savage spectacle," Brutus said. "Our reasons are so full of serious consideration that, Antony, even if you were the son of Caesar, you would be persuaded that we had justly killed Caesar."

"That is all I seek," Mark Antony said, "and I ask that I be allowed to take Caesar's corpse to the Forum, and I ask that on the speakers' platform, as becomes a friend, I be allowed to speak at Caesar's funeral."

"You shall, Mark Antony," Brutus said.

Cassius said, "Brutus, may I have a word with you?"

Brutus and Cassius went a short distance away from Mark Antony, and Cassius said, "You do not know what you are doing. Do not allow Antony to speak at Caesar's funeral. Don't you realize how much the people may be moved by Antony's speech?"

"I beg your pardon," Brutus said. "I myself will speak first, and I will explain the reasons why Caesar had to die. Before Antony speaks, I will say that he speaks by our leave and with our permission, and that we want Caesar to have all the proper funeral rites and lawful ceremonies. This shall do us more good than harm."

"I am afraid of what may happen," Cassius said. "I am against Antony's speaking at Caesar's funeral."

Brutus said, "Mark Antony, here, take Caesar's body. You shall not in your funeral speech blame us. Instead, speak all the good you can of Caesar, and say you do it with our permission, or else you shall not have any hand at all in his funeral. You shall speak on the same speakers' platform where I am going now, and you shall speak after I have finished my speech."

"So be it," Mark Antony said. "I desire no more than that."

"Prepare the body then, and follow us."

Everyone, except for Mark Antony, left.

Kneeling by the corpse of Caesar, Mark Antony said, "Pardon me, you bleeding piece of earth, that I am meek and gentle with these butchers! You are the ruins of the noblest man who ever lived in the tide of times — the ebb and flow of history. Woe to the hands that shed this valuable blood! I now prophesy over your wounds, which, like speechless mouths, open their ruby lips, to ask my tongue to speak. I prophesy that a curse shall light upon the bodies of men. Domestic fury and fierce civil strife shall paralyze all the parts of Italy. Blood and destruction shall be so common and dreadful objects shall be so familiar that mothers shall only smile when they see their infants cut to pieces by the hands of war. All pity will disappear because people are so accustomed to witnessing deadly deeds. Caesar's spirit, searching for revenge, with Ate — the Roman goddess of vengeance coming hot from Hell — by his side, shall in these territories with a monarch's voice cry 'Havoc,' and let loose the dogs of war. This foul deed shall result in men becoming stinking carrion above the earth, groaning for burial."

A servant came toward Mark Antony.

"You serve Octavius Caesar, don't you?" Mark Antony asked.

Octavius Caesar was the grand-nephew and adopted heir of Julius Caesar, to whom Calpurnia had given no children.

"I do, Mark Antony."

"Julius Caesar wrote for him to come to Rome."

"Octavius Caesar received his letters, and he is coming. He told me to say to you by word of mouth —"

The servant saw the corpse of Julius Caesar and exclaimed, "Oh, Caesar!"

"Your heart is big," Mark Antony said. "Go away a short distance and cry. Sorrow, I see, is catching. My eyes, seeing those tears of sorrow in your eyes, have started to cry. Is your master coming?"

"He will sleep tonight within 21 miles of Rome."

"Go back to him quickly," Mark Antony said, "and tell him what has happened. Here is a mourning Rome, a dangerous Rome, not a Rome of safety for Octavius yet. Hurry now, and tell him. But wait. Stay here for a while. You shall not return to Octavius until I have carried this corpse into the Forum. In my speech, I shall see how the people take the assassination of Caesar by these bloody men. You shall report back to Octavius what happens.

"Now help me to carry Caesar's body."

The two men carried Caesar's body to the Forum where the funeral orations would be given.

— 3.2 —

In the Forum were Brutus, Cassius, and many common citizens of Rome.

The citizens shouted, "We will be satisfied! Let us be given a satisfactory explanation!"

"Then follow me," Brutus said, "and listen to what I have to say, friends."

He added, "Cassius, you go to the other street. Let us divide the audience. Half will hear you speak, and half will hear me speak."

He said to the citizens, "Those who will hear me speak, let them stay here. Those who will follow Cassius, go with him. Here in public, we will tell you the reasons why Caesar had to die."

The first citizen said, "I will hear Brutus speak."

Another citizen said, "I will hear Cassius speak, and we will compare their reasons after we have heard both Brutus and Cassius speak."

Cassius left, and several citizens followed him to hear him speak.

Brutus went to the speakers' platform.

The third citizen said, "The noble Brutus has ascended to the speakers' platform. Silence!"

"Be patient until the end of my speech," Brutus said. "Romans, countrymen, and friends! Hear me explain my reasons for killing Caesar, and be silent so that you can hear me. Believe me because of my honor. Have respect for my honor so that you may believe me. Use your wisdom to critique what I say, and use your intelligence so that you may the better judge me.

"If there is in this assembly any dear friend of Caesar's, to him I say that Brutus' love for Caesar was no less than his. If then that friend demands why Brutus rose against Caesar, this is my answer: Not that I loved Caesar less, but that I loved Rome more. Would you prefer that Caesar were living and that you all die as slaves, or would you prefer that Caesar were dead so that you can all live as free men? As Caesar loved me, I weep for him. As he was successful in war, I rejoice at it. As he was valiant, I honor him. But as he was ambitious, I slew him. Caesar has received tears for his love, joy for his success in war, honor for his valor, and death for his ambition. Who is here so base that he wants to be a slave? If any of you are like that, speak up, because that man have I offended. Who is here so barbarous that he would prefer not to be a Roman? If any of you are like that, speak up, because that man have I offended. Who is here so vile that he will not love his country? If any of you are like that, speak up, because that man have I offended. I pause for a reply."

The citizens shouted, "None of us is like that, Brutus."

"Then I have offended no one," Brutus said, "I have done no more to Caesar than you would do to me if I were to become a tyrant. The reasons for Caesar's death are recorded on a roll of parchment in the Capitol. Caesar's glory is not belittled when he has earned it, and neither are his offenses, for which he suffered death, exaggerated."

Mark Antony and others arrived, carrying Caesar's body.

Brutus said, "Here comes his body, mourned by Mark Antony, who, though he had no hand in Caesar's death, shall receive the benefit of Caesar's dying: a place in the commonwealth, just as each of you has.

"With these final words, I depart: I slew my best friend for the good of Rome, and I still possess the dagger that killed him. I will use it to kill myself when my country needs my death."

The Roman citizens shouted, "Live, Brutus! Live! Live!"

The first citizen shouted, "Let us carry Brutus in triumph home to his house."

The second citizen shouted, "Let us create a statue of him and place it among the statues of his ancestors."

The third citizen shouted, "Let him be Caesar and rule us."

The fourth citizen shouted, "Caesar's better qualities shall be crowned in Brutus!"

The first citizen shouted, "We'll bring him to his house with shouts and clamors."

Brutus began, "My countrymen —"

The second citizen shouted, "Peace, silence! Brutus speaks."

The first citizen shouted, "Quiet!"

"Good countrymen, let me depart alone," Brutus said. "And, for my sake, stay here with Antony. Honor Caesar's corpse, and listen to Antony's speech about Caesar's glories. Mark Antony, by our permission, is allowed to make this funeral speech. I ask you to stay and listen to him. Not a man should depart, except for myself, until after Antony has spoken."

Brutus left.

The first citizen said, "Let us stay and hear Mark Antony speak."

The third citizen said, "Let him go up onto the speakers' platform. We will listen to him. Noble Antony, go up and speak."

Mary Antony said, "I am indebted to you, thanks to Brutus," as he climbed onto the speakers' platform.

The fourth citizen asked, "What did he say about Brutus?"

The third citizen said, "He said that he is indebted to all of us, thanks to Brutus."

The fourth citizen said, "If he is wise, he will speak no harm of Brutus here."

The first citizen said, "Julius Caesar was a tyrant."

The third citizen said, "That's for certain. We are blessed that Rome is rid of him."

The second citizen said, "Quiet. Let us hear what Antony has to say."

"You gentle Romans —" Mark Antony shouted above the noise.

The citizens shouted, "Quiet! Let us hear him!"

"Friends, Romans, countrymen, lend me your ears," Mark Antony said. "I come to bury Caesar, not to praise him. The evil that men do lives after them; the good is often buried with their bones. So let it be with Caesar. The noble Brutus has told you that Caesar was ambitious. If this is true, it was a grievous fault, and grievously has Caesar answered for it. Here, with the permission of Brutus and the rest of the conspirators — for Brutus is an honorable man, and so are they all, all honorable men — I have come to speak at Caesar's funeral. Caesar was my friend, faithful and just to me. But Brutus says he was ambitious, and Brutus is an honorable man. Caesar brought many captives home to Rome, and the money paid to ransom them filled the public treasury. Did this in Caesar seem ambitious? When the poor have cried, Caesar has wept. Ambition should be made of sterner stuff. Yet Brutus says he was ambitious, and Brutus is an honorable man. You all did see that on the Lupercal I three times presented Caesar with a Kingly crown, which he did three times refuse. Was this ambition? Yet Brutus says Caesar was ambitious, and, to be sure, Brutus is an honorable man. I speak not to disprove what Brutus spoke, but I am here to speak what I do know. You all did love him once, not without cause. What cause then keeps you from mourning for him? Oh, Reason, you have fled to brutish beasts, and men have lost their reason. Bear with me. My heart is in the coffin there with Caesar, and I must pause until it comes back to me."

The first citizen said, "I think that there is much sense in what Antony says."

"If you think correctly about this, Caesar has been done great wrong," the second citizen said.

"Has he, friends?" the third citizen said. "Then I fear that a worse man will replace him."

"Did you hear what Antony said?" the fourth citizen asked. "Caesar would not take the crown; therefore, we can be certain that he was not ambitious."

"If Caesar was not ambitious, then some people are going to pay for his death," the first citizen said.

"Poor soul!" the second citizen said. "Antony's eyes are as red as fire from crying."

"There's not a nobler man in Rome than Antony," the third citizen said.

"Now let us listen to him — he begins again to speak," the fourth citizen said.

"Only yesterday the word of Caesar might have overcome the opposition of the world," Antony said. "Now he lies there, and no one has the humility to show him respect. Friends, if I were disposed to stir your hearts and minds to mutiny and rage, I would do Brutus wrong and Cassius wrong, who, you all know, are honorable men. I will not do them wrong. I instead choose to wrong the dead, to wrong myself and you, rather than wrong such honorable men. But here's a parchment document with the seal of Caesar that I found in his study. It is his will. If you could hear his will and testament — which, pardon me, I do not intend to read out loud — you would go and kiss dead Caesar's wounds and dip your handkerchiefs in his sacred blood. Indeed, you would even beg for one of his hairs as a memento, and, dying, you would mention it in your wills, and bequeath it as a rich legacy to your children."

"We will hear the will," the fourth citizen shouted. "Read it out loud, Mark Antony!"

"The will, the will!" the citizens shouted. "We will hear Caesar's will!"

"Have patience, gentle friends," Antony said. "I must not read Caesar's will out loud. It is not fitting that you know how much Caesar loved you. You are not wood, you are not stones, you are men. Being men, hearing the will of Caesar will inflame you — it will make you mad. It is good you do not know that you are his heirs, for, if you did, what would come of it!"

"Read the will!" the fourth citizen shouted. "We'll hear it, Antony! You shall read us the will — Caesar's will!"

"Will you be patient?" Antony asked. "Will you stay awhile? I said too much when I told you about Caesar's will. I fear that I wrong the honorable men whose daggers have stabbed Caesar — I do fear it."

"They were traitors!" the fourth citizen shouted, adding scornfully, "Honorable men!"

The citizens shouted, "The will! Caesar's last will and testament!"

"The conspirators were villains, murderers!" the second citizen shouted. "The will! Read the will out loud!"

"You will compel me, then, to read the will?" Antony said. "Then make a ring about the corpse of Caesar, and let me show you him who made the will. Shall I descend from the speakers' platform? Will you give me permission to descend?"

"Come down," several citizens said.

"Descend," the second citizen said.

"You have our permission," the third citizen said.

Mark Antony came down from the speakers' platform and stood over Caesar's corpse.

"Make a ring around Caesar's corpse," the fourth citizen said. "Stand around the corpse."

"Stand back from the bier," the first citizen said. "Stand back from the body."

"Give Antony, most noble Antony, room," the second citizen said.

"Do not crowd me," Antony said. "Stand farther away."

"Stand back. Give him room. Fall back," several citizens said.

"If you have tears, prepare to shed them now," Antony said, touching Caesar's cloak. "You all know this cloak. I remember the first time that Caesar put it on. It was on a summer's evening, in his tent, that day he conquered the Nervii, enemies of Rome who lived in northern Gaul.

"Look! In this place ran Cassius' dagger through. See what a rent the malicious Casca made. Through this the well-beloved Brutus stabbed, and as he plucked his cursed steel away, see how the blood of Caesar followed it, as if it were rushing out of doors to find out if it were Brutus who so unkindly knocked, because Brutus, as you know, was Caesar's angel — Caesar trusted Brutus as if Brutus were his guardian angel. Judge, gods, how dearly Caesar loved Brutus! This was the cruelest and most unkindest cut of all because when the noble Caesar saw him stab, ingratitude, which is stronger than traitors' weapons, quite vanquished Caesar. That is when Caesar's mighty heart burst. Caesar covered his face with his cloak and at the base of Pompey's statue, on which was splashed Caesar's blood, great Caesar fell. What a fall was there, my countrymen! At that time, I, and you, and all of us fell down, while bloody treason triumphed over us."

The Roman citizens wept, and Antony said, "Oh, now you weep, and I see that you feel the blow of pity. These are gracious tears. Kind souls, you are crying when you see only the wounded cloak of Caesar. Look now!"

With a swift movement, Antony uncovered Caesar's corpse and said, "Here is Caesar himself, marred, as you see, with the wounds of traitors."

"Oh, pitiful sight!" the first citizen said.

"Oh, noble Caesar!" the second citizen said.

"Oh, woeful day!" the third citizen said.

"Oh, traitors, villains!" the fourth citizen said.

"Oh, most bloody sight!" the first citizen said.

"We will be revenged," the second citizen said.

"Revenge! Go! Seek! Burn! Fire! Kill! Slay! Let not a traitor live!" the citizens shouted.

"Wait, countrymen," Antony said.

"Quiet!" the first citizen shouted. "Let us hear the noble Antony!"

"We'll hear him, we'll follow him, we'll die with him," the second citizen shouted.

"Good friends, sweet friends, let me not stir you up to such a sudden flood of mutiny," Antony said. "These men who have done this deed are honorable. I don't know what personal grievances they had against Caesar that made them kill him. These men are wise and honorable, and will, no doubt, answer you with reasons for why they killed Caesar. I come not, friends, to steal away your hearts: I am not an orator, as Brutus is. As all of you know, I am a plain and blunt man, who loves my friend. These men who gave me permission to speak about Caesar know that I am no orator. I have neither intellectual cleverness, nor rhetorical skill, nor authority, nor rhetorical gestures, nor eloquence, nor the power of speech to stir up the blood of men. I only speak directly and to the point. I tell you that which you yourselves do know. I show you sweet Caesar's wounds — those poor dumb mouths — and I ask them to speak for me, but if I were Brutus, and Brutus were Antony, then Antony would have the rhetorical power to enrage your spirits and make every wound of Caesar speak so that even the stones of Rome would rise and mutiny and riot."

"We'll riot," the Roman citizens said.

"We'll burn the house of Brutus," the first citizen said.

"Let's go!" the third citizen said. "Let's find the conspirators!"

"Wait, countrymen," Antony said. "Listen to me."

"Quiet!" the citizens shouted. "Hear what Antony, most noble Antony, has to say!"

"Why, friends, you go to do you not know what," Antony said. "Why does Caesar deserve your love and respect? You do not know yet. Therefore, I must tell you. You have forgotten the will I told you of."

"That's true," the citizens said. "The will! Let's stay and hear the will!"

"Here is the will in my hand," Antony said, "and it bears Caesar's seal. To every Roman citizen he gives — to each man — seventy-five drachmas."

"Most noble Caesar!" the second citizen said. "We'll revenge his death!"

"Oh, royal Caesar!" the third citizen shouted.

"Hear me patiently," Antony said.

"Quiet!" the citizens shouted.

"In addition, Caesar has left you all his gardens, his private summer houses, and newly planted orchards, on this side of the Tiber River," Antony said. "He has left them to you and to your heirs forever. They will be public pleasure gardens in which you can walk and relax. Here was a Caesar! When will there come another like him!"

"Never, never!" the first citizen shouted. "Let's go! We'll cremate Caesar's corpse in the holy place and then with the firebrands set fire to the traitors' houses. Let's carry Caesar's corpse to the holy place!"

"Fetch fire!" the second citizen said.

"Tear apart benches for wood!" the third citizen said.

"Tear apart shutters and anything we can use for wood to burn," the fourth citizen said.

The citizens departed, carrying Caesar's corpse.

"Now let it work," Antony said. "Troubles and riots, you have started. Take whatever course you will."

A servant came up to Mark Antony, who asked, "What news do you have for me?"

"Sir, Octavius has already come to Rome."

"Where is he?" Antony asked.

"He and the soldier Lepidus are at Julius Caesar's house."

"And there I will immediately go to visit him," Antony said. "He comes just as I had wished. The goddess Fortune is merry, and in this mood she will give us anything."

"I heard him say that Brutus and Cassius have ridden like madmen through the gates of Rome."

"Probably they have heard that the people are rioting because I persuaded them to riot," Antony said. "Take me to Octavius."

— 3.3 —

Cinna the poet — not Cinna the conspirator — walked alone on a street in Rome. The poet was named Helvius Cinna; the conspirator was named Cornelius Cinna.

Cinna said to himself, "I dreamt last night that I feasted with Caesar, and bad omens now weigh on my imagination. I have no wish to wander out of doors, and yet something leads me forth."

A mob of citizens arrived.

"What is your name?" the first citizen asked Cinna.

"Where are you going?" the second citizen asked.

"Where do you live?" the third citizen asked.

"Are you a married man or a bachelor?" the fourth citizen asked.

"Answer every man directly," the second citizen said.

"Yes, and briefly," the first citizen said.

"Yes, and wisely," the fourth citizen said.

"Yes, and truly — you had better!" the third citizen said.

"What is my name?" Cinna the poet repeated. "Where am I going? Where do I live? Am I a married man or a bachelor? Then, to answer every man directly and briefly, wisely and truly — wisely I say, I am a bachelor."

"That's as much as to say that they who marry are fools — you'll get a blow from me for saying that, I think," the second citizen said. "Now answer us directly."

"Directly, I am going to Caesar's funeral," Cinna the poet said.

"As a friend or as an enemy?" the first citizen said.

"As a friend," Cinna the poet said.

"That matter is answered directly," the second citizen said.

"Where do you live — briefly?" the fourth citizen asked.

"Briefly, I live by the Capitol," Cinna the poet said.

"What is your name, sir, truly?" the third citizen asked.

"Truly, my name is Cinna."

"Tear him to pieces! He's a conspirator!" the first citizen shouted.

"I am Cinna the poet! I am Cinna the poet!"

"Tear him to pieces because of his bad verses!" the fourth citizen shouted.

"I am not Cinna the conspirator!"

"It does not matter — his name's Cinna," the fourth citizen said. "Pluck his name out of his heart, and let the rest of him go."

"Tear him to pieces!" the third citizen cried.

The mob killed Cinna the poet.

"Let's carry firebrands to Brutus' house and to Cassius' house and burn them down!" the third citizen shouted. "Some of us will go to Decius' house, and some to Casca's house and some to Ligarius' house. Let's go!"

CHAPTER 4

— 4.1 —

In a house in Rome, Antony, Octavius, and Lepidus were seated at a table. They had joined together to seize power and to divide the Roman territory into three parts — Europe, Asia, and Africa — that they would rule separately. Currently, they were making a list of people in Rome who would die. By killing many men, and exiling others, they hoped to stop opposition.

Mark Antony had a wax tablet in his hands. In the wax were written many names. Whenever they decided that a man had to die, Antony made a mark by that person's name.

"These men, then, shall die," Antony said. "Their names are pricked."

Octavius said to Lepidus, "Your brother also must die. Do you consent, Lepidus?"

"I do consent —" Lepidus began.

"Make a mark by his name, Antony," Octavius said.

Lepidus continued, "— on the condition that Publius — your sister's son, Mark Antony — shall not live."

"He shall not live," Antony agreed. "Look, with a mark I damn him to die. But, Lepidus, go to Caesar's house. Bring his will here, and we shall alter it to reduce his legacies and keep money for ourselves."

"Will you two be here?" Lepidus asked.

"We will be either here or at the Capitol," Octavius said.

Lepidus left.

Antony said, "Lepidus is an insignificant and undeserving man who is fit only for running errands. Is it fitting that when we divide the Roman territory into three parts — Europe, Asia, and Africa — that he get one of those parts?"

"You have thought him worthy," Octavius said. "And you allowed him to vote on who should die in our harsh sentences of death and of exile."

"Octavius, I have seen more days than you. I am older and more experienced," Antony said. "It is true that we are laying honors on Lepidus so that he can bear the burden of our unpopular actions that shall give us power. He — not us — will be blamed for them. He shall bear the load of honors we give him as the ass bears gold. He will groan and sweat under the load, he will be

52

driven or led where we want him to go, and when he has brought our treasure where we want it to be, then we will unload the treasure and set him loose, like an ass without a burden, to shake his ears and to graze in a pasture."

"You may do as you like," Octavius said, "but he is a tried and valiant soldier."

"So is my horse, Octavius, and because of that I do give him his feed. My horse is a creature that I teach to fight, to turn, to stop, to run directly on — I guide his bodily motion. And, to some extent, so is Lepidus. He must be taught and trained and bid to go forth. He is a barren-spirited fellow — he has no ideas of his own. He feeds on curiosities, artifices, and fashions or styles. He becomes interested in things only after they are out of date. So do not talk about Lepidus except as a tool whom we may use.

"But now, Octavius, listen to important matters. Brutus and Cassius are raising armies. We must immediately raise our own armies and march against them. Therefore, let our forces be combined into one army, and let us get support from our allies and friends, and make the most of our resources. We need to immediately go into council and decide how we can uncover secret plans and how we can best fight open dangers."

"Let us do so," Octavius said. "We are like a bear that is tied to a stake, and surrounded by baying enemies. And some people who smile at us, I fear, have in their hearts millions of mischiefs."

— 4.2 —

In a camp near Sardis in western Turkey, in front of Brutus' tent, Brutus, Lucilius, Lucius, and some soldiers met Titinius and Pindarus. Titinius was a friend to Brutus and Cassius, and Pindarus was one of Cassius' slaves.

Brutus cried, "Halt!"

Lucilius cried, "Pass on the order to the troops to halt!"

"How are you, Lucilius?" Brutus asked. "Is Cassius near?"

"He is near," Lucilius replied. "Pindarus has come to bring you greetings from him."

"Cassius has sent a good man to greet me," Brutus said.

He said to Pindarus, "Your master, because of some change in himself, or because of the bad conduct of some of his officers, has given me some good reasons to wish that some things that have been done, had not been done. But, if he is near, he will be able to talk to me and explain things."

"I do not doubt but that my noble master will appear, as usual, deserving of respect and honor," Pindarus said.

"I do not doubt it," Brutus said.

He added, "Lucilius, tell me how Cassius greeted you."

"He received me with courtesy and with respect enough," Lucilius said, "but not with such evidence of close friendship nor with such free and friendly conversation as he has displayed in the past."

"You have described a hot friend cooling," Brutus said. "It is always the case, Lucilius, that when friendship begins to sicken and decay, the friend treats you with an unnatural politeness. Plain and simple friendship is not deceitful or phony. But hollow, insincere men, like horses eager to run before the race begins, make a big show and promise of their spirit, but when the race begins, they lose their spirit and like deceiving and worthless nags, they cease to run."

He added, "Is Cassius' army coming here?"

"His army intends to camp in Sardis tonight," Lucilius answered. "The greater part — including all the cavalry — is coming with Cassius."

"Look," Brutus said. "Cassius has arrived. Let us march at a dignified pace and meet him."

Cassius cried, "Halt!"

Brutus cried, "Halt! Pass the order down the line of soldiers."

"Halt!" the first soldier cried.

"Halt!" the second soldier cried.

"Halt!" the third soldier cried.

Cassius was angry. He said to Brutus, "Most noble brother, you have done me wrong."

"May the gods judge me," Brutus replied. "Do I wrong my enemies? No! So how could I wrong a brother?"

"Brutus, this dignified manner of yours hides wrongs. And when you do them —"

Brutus interrupted, "Cassius, calm down. Speak about your grievances quietly. I know you well. The eyes of both our armies here should perceive nothing but friendship between us, so let us not argue in public. We will order the soldiers to move away a little, and then in my tent, Cassius, you can tell me about your grievances."

"Pindarus, order our commanders to lead their soldiers a little distance away from here," Cassius ordered.

"Lucilius, you do the same," Brutus said. "Let no man come to our tent until Cassius and I have finished our conference. Order Lucius and Titinius to guard our door."

— 4.3 —

Inside Brutus' tent, Brutus and Cassius argued.

"Here is a way that you have wronged me," Cassius said. "You have found guilty and publicly disgraced Lucius Pella for taking bribes here from the Sardians. I sent you letters on behalf of Lucius Pella because I know the man, and you ignored my letters."

"You wronged yourself to write letters in behalf of such a man," Brutus said.

"In such a time as this, it is not suitable for every trivial offence to get its punishment," Cassius said.

"Let me tell you, Cassius, you yourself are much condemned for having an itchy palm — for selling and trading official positions for gold to people who do not deserve such positions."

"I have an itchy palm!" Cassius said. "You are Brutus who speaks this; if you were not Brutus, I swear by the gods, this speech would be your last."

"Your name, Cassius, protects this corruption by giving it an appearance of respectability, and therefore it goes unpunished," Brutus said.

"Unpunished!"

"Remember the Ides of March," Brutus said. "Did not great Julius Caesar bleed for the sake of justice? Who among us stabbed Caesar except in the cause of justice? We struck the foremost man of the entire world because he allowed robbers to go free. Shall we now contaminate our fingers with base bribes? Shall we sell the vast capacity we have for being honorable so we can acquire the trash and money that may be grasped by taking bribes? I would prefer to be a dog, and howl at the Moon, than to be such a Roman."

"Brutus, do not provoke me," Cassius said. "I will not endure it. You forget yourself when you hedge me in with your rules and limit my freedom of action. I am a soldier. I am more experienced and abler than yourself to make treaties."

"No, you are not, Cassius."

"I am."

"I say you are not."

55

"Test my patience no more, or I shall forget myself," Cassius said. "Be concerned about your health, and tempt me no further."

"Go away, insignificant man!" Brutus said.

"Is it possible that you can say that to me?" Cassius asked.

"Listen to me, for I will speak," Brutus said. "Am I required to give way to your rash anger? Shall I be frightened when a madman stares at me?"

"Gods, must I endure all this?"

"All this?" Brutus said. "Yes, and more. Rage until your proud heart breaks. Go and show your slaves how angry you are, and make your slaves tremble. Must I give in to you? Must I show respectful attention to you? Must I stand here and cringe because you are in a testy mood? By the gods, you shall digest the poison of your temper, even though it makes you burst. From this day on, I'll use you for my entertainment — I will laugh at you when you are hotheaded."

"Has it come to this?" Cassius said.

"You say you are a better soldier," Brutus said. "Prove it. Make your boasting come true, and I shall be well pleased. For my own part, I shall be glad to learn from noble men."

"You wrong me in every way," Cassius said. "You wrong me, Brutus. I said, an elder soldier, not a better. Did I say 'better'?"

"If you did, I don't care," Brutus said.

"When Julius Caesar was alive, he would not have dared to have angered me in this way."

"Be quiet," Brutus said. "You would not have dared to provoke his anger."

"I would not have dared!" Cassius said.

"No."

"What? Dared not to provoke him!"

"No, because you would fear for your life," Brutus replied.

"Don't take my friendship for you for granted. I may do something that I shall be sorry for."

"You have already done something that you should be sorry for — you have taken bribes," Brutus said. "There is no terror, Cassius, in your threats. I am not afraid of them because I am so secure in my honesty and integrity that your threats pass by me like the idle wind, which I do not fear or respect.

"I sent to you to tell you to send me certain sums of gold, which you denied me. I can raise no money by vile means."

An impartial observer might think about these things: Brutus can raise no money by vile means. Is it OK for Cassius to raise money by vile means and then give the money to Brutus? Is it OK for Cassius to raise money by accepting bribes and then give the money to Brutus? What if the only way to raise money is through vile means?

"By Heaven," Brutus continued, "I had rather turn my heart and the drops of my blood into money than to wring from the hard hands of peasants their vile coins by tricks and deceitful means. I sent to you for gold to pay my legions of soldiers, and you denied me that money. Was that done like Cassius? Would I have done that to you? When Marcus Brutus grows so greedy as to keep such wretched bits of metal from his friends, then be ready, gods, with all your thunderbolts — dash me to pieces!"

"I did not deny you the money."

"You did."

"I did not," Cassius said. "He who brought my answer back to you was a fool. Brutus, you have broken my heart. A friend should put up with his friend's weaknesses, but you make my weaknesses greater than they are."

"I do not until you inflict your weaknesses on me."

"You no longer like me."

"I do not like your faults."

"A friendly eye could never see such faults," Cassius said.

"A flatterer's eye would not, even if they should appear to be as huge as the high mountain that is Olympus."

"Come to me, Antony and young Octavius, come," Cassius said. "Revenge yourselves alone on Cassius because Cassius is weary of the world. He is hated by one he loves, defied by his brother, rebuked like a slave. All my faults are observed, written down in a notebook, learned by heart, and memorized so that they can be thrown in my teeth. I could weep my spirit from my eyes and die of grief! There is my dagger, and here is my naked breast. Within is a heart more precious than the mine of Plutus, the god of riches. My heart is richer than gold. If you are a Roman, cut my heart out. I, who denied you gold, will give you my heart. Strike me like you struck at Caesar because I know that when you hated him the worst, you loved him better than you ever loved Cassius."

"Sheathe your dagger," Brutus said. "Be angry whenever you will — your anger shall have free expression. Do what you will — I will take your abuse as a mere whim or bad mood. Cassius, you are yoked — partners — with a lamb that carries anger like the flint carries fire. When the flint is struck hard, it shows a hasty spark, and then immediately is cold again. So it is with anger and me."

"Has Cassius lived to be only mirth and laughter — a joke — to Brutus, when grief and anger vex him?"

"When I said that, I was ill-tempered, too."

"Do you admit it?" Cassius said. "Give me your hand."

They shook hands.

"I give you my heart, too," Brutus said.

"Oh, Brutus!"

"What's the matter?"

"Aren't you friendly enough to bear with me, when my bad temper, which I inherited from my mother, makes me forget how I should behave?"

"Yes, Cassius. From henceforth, whenever you are angry at Brutus, he will think your mother is angry, and leave it at that."

Despite their precautions, gossip about their argument had spread among the soldiers, and now a poet came to Brutus' tent and demanded to talk to Brutus and Cassius. The poet did not know that Brutus and Cassius had already patched up their quarrel.

The poet said, "Let me go in to see the generals. There is some argument between them, and they ought not to be alone together."

Lucilius, one of the guards outside Brutus' tent, said, "You shall not go to them."

The poet replied, "Nothing but death shall stop me."

The poet entered the tent, followed by Lucilius, Titinius, and Lucius.

"What is this!" Cassius said. "What is the matter?"

"For shame, you generals!" the poet said. "What do you mean? Love each other, and be friends, as two such men as you should be. I have seen more years, I'm sure, than either of ye."

Brutus and Cassius made fun of the poet, although older men ought to be respected.

"Ha!" Cassius said. "How vilely does this rude man rhyme!"

"Get out of here," Brutus said. "Saucy fellow, go!"

"Bear with him, Brutus," Cassius said. "This is just the way he is."

"I will allow him to be eccentric when he realizes that there is a proper time and place for it," Brutus said. "What place has war for these idiot rhymesters?"

He said to the poet, "Get out!"

The poet left.

"Lucilius and Titinius, order the commanders to prepare to pitch camp for their companies tonight," Brutus ordered.

Cassius ordered, "Then return immediately to us — and bring Messala with you."

Lucilius and Titinius left to carry out their orders.

"Lucius, bring us a bowl of wine," Brutus ordered.

Lucius left to carry out his errand.

"I did not think you could have been so angry," Cassius said.

"Oh, Cassius, I am sick with many griefs."

"If you surrender to the chance evils that befall us, you are not making use of your Stoic philosophy that ought to teach us to bear such evils patiently and without complaining."

"No man bears sorrow better than I do," Brutus said. "Portia is dead."

"Portia?"

"She is dead."

"How did I escape your killing me when I quarreled with you?" Cassius asked. "This is an unbearable loss of someone who touched and loved you! From which illness did she die?"

"Unable to endure my absence, and grieving because young Octavius and Mark Antony have made themselves so powerful — news of their power arrived with news of her death — she despaired and, while her servants were absent, she put hot coals in her mouth and swallowed fire."

"That is how she died?"

"Yes."

"Oh, you immortal gods!"

Lucius returned, carrying wine and a candle.

"Speak no more about her," Brutus said to Cassius. "Give me a bowl of wine. With this drink, I bury all unkindness between us, Cassius."

He drank.

"My heart is thirsty for peace between us," Cassius said.

He added, "Fill the cup, Lucius, until the wine overfills it. I cannot drink too much of Brutus' love."

He drank.

Brutus heard approaching footsteps and said, "Come in, Titinius!"

Lucius left, and both Titinius and Messala entered Brutus' tent.

"Welcome, good Messala," Brutus said. "Now let us sit around this candle here, and discuss our needs."

"Portia, are you really gone?" Cassius said to himself.

"No more, please," Brutus said to Cassius.

He added, "Messala, I have here received letters that state that young Octavius and Mark Antony are marching against us with a mighty army. They are marching toward Philippi, a city in northeastern Greece."

"I have letters that say the same thing," Messala replied.

"Do they say anything else?" Brutus asked.

"That by proclamation of the death sentence and bills of outlawry, Octavius, Antony, and Lepidus have put to death a hundred Senators. They were declared outlaws and their property was seized."

"There our letters do not agree well," Brutus said. "My letters speak of seventy Senators who have died because of their proscriptions. Cicero is one of those who died."

"Cicero!" Cassius said.

"Cicero is dead by order of Octavius, Mark Antony, and Lepidus," Messala said.

He then asked Brutus, "Have you received any letters from your wife, my lord?"

"No, Messala."

"Have any of the letters you have received contained news about her?"

Brutus did not want to talk about his late wife. He replied again, "No, Messala."

"That is strange, I think," Messala said.

"Why are you asking about her? Have you heard anything about her in the letters you have received?" Brutus asked.

"No, my lord."

Brutus decided that eventually he would have to talk about his late wife, so he might as well start now. He said to Messala, "Now, as you are a Roman, tell me the truth."

"Then like a Roman bear the truth I tell you. It is certain that she is dead and that she died in a strange manner."

To a close friend such as Cassius, Brutus could reveal his feelings. In front of other people, he would act like a Stoic philosopher. He said, "Why, farewell, Portia. We must die, Messala. I have known that she must die one day, and so I have the patience to endure her death now."

"Just like you are doing now, great men should endure great losses," Messala said.

"I also know Stoic philosophy," Cassius said. "But yet I could not bear such a great loss as patiently as you are bearing it."

"Well, let us return to the work we must do while we are alive," Brutus said. "What do you think about marching to Philippi immediately?"

"I do not think it is a good idea," Cassius said.

"Why not?" Brutus asked.

"It is better that the enemy come to us. That way, he will exhaust his supplies and weary his soldiers, doing himself harm, while we, staying here, will be full of rest, in a good defensive position, and fresh."

"Good reasons must, of necessity, give way to better reasons," Brutus said. "The people between Philippi and here have been forced to help us. They have only grudgingly given us supplies. Our enemy's army, marching through them, shall increase as people join the army. They will march against us refreshed, with newly added soldiers, and encouraged by the people's support. We can stop these advantages for their army if we march to and fight at Philippi. Those people who would support our enemy will be cut off from our enemy's army."

"Listen to me, good brother," Cassius started to object.

"Pardon me," Brutus said. "I am not finished. You must know that we have gotten all that our allies can give us. Our armies are large, and our cause is at its peak. The enemy armies grow larger every day; they have not yet peaked. We are at our peak and are ready to decline. There is a tide in the affairs of men, which, taken at the flood, leads on to fortune. Neglected, all the voyage of their life is bound in shallows and in miseries. On such a full sea are we now afloat, and we must take the current when it serves, or lose our ventures. Now is the time for us to take action and march against our enemies, not to sit back and let our enemies come to us."

"Then, as you wish, march to meet them," Cassius said. "My army and I will also march and meet them at Philippi."

"The deepest part of night has crept upon our talk," Brutus said. "We must obey natural necessity and get at least a little sleep. Is there anything else we should talk about?"

"No," Cassius said. "Good night. Early tomorrow we will rise and march to Philippi."

"Lucius!" Brutus called.

Lucius appeared.

"Bring me my robe."

Brutus added, "Farewell, good Messala. Good night, Titinius. Noble, noble Cassius, good night to you, and sleep well."

"My dear brother!" Cassius said. "This night began badly. May there never again come such division between our souls, Brutus!"

Lucius appeared, carrying Brutus' robe.

"All is well," Brutus said.

"Good night, my lord," Cassius said.

"Good night, good brother," Brutus said.

Titinius and Messala said, "Good night, Lord Brutus."

"Farewell, everyone," Brutus said.

Everyone except Brutus and Lucius left.

"Give me my robe," Brutus said. "Where is your lute?"

"Here in the tent," Lucius said.

"I can tell by the way you speak that you are sleepy," Brutus said. "Poor boy, I don't blame you. You are tired because you have been kept awake so long. Call Claudius and one other of my men. I'll have them sleep on cushions in my tent in case I need them."

"Varro and Claudius!" Lucius called.

Varro and Claudius entered Brutus' tent.

Varro asked, "Does my lord need me?"

"Please, sirs, lie in my tent and sleep," Brutus said. "It may happen that I shall wake you by and by to carry a message to my brother Cassius."

"If it is OK with you, we will stand and wait here until you need us," Varro said.

"No," Brutus said. "Lie down and sleep, good sirs. Perhaps I shall not need you."

Brutus put his hand in the pocket of the robe that Lucius had brought to him and said, "Look, Lucius, here's the book I have been looking for. I put it in the pocket of my robe."

Varro and Claudius lay down to sleep.

"I was sure your lordship did not give the book to me," Lucius said.

"Bear with me, good boy," Brutus said. "I am very forgetful. If you can stay awake a while, will you play a tune or two on your lute?"

"Yes, my lord, if you want me to," Lucius said.

"I do, my boy. I trouble you too much, but I am grateful that you are willing to play for me."

"It is my duty, sir."

"I ought not to make you do more than you can do," Brutus said. "I know that young boys need their rest."

"I have slept for a while, my lord, already."

"That was well done, and you shall sleep again. I will not hold you long," Brutus said. "If I live through this, I will be good to you."

Lucius played and sang a song. But he was tired and fell asleep.

"This is a sleepy tune," Brutus said. "Oh, murderous slumber, you have arrested this boy's playing and made him sleep although he was playing music. Gentle boy, good night. I will not do you wrong and wake you. You might break your lute, and so I will take it from you and put it here, where it will be safe, and so, good boy, good night."

He looked at his book and said, "Let me see. Isn't the corner of the page turned down where I stopped reading? Here it is, I think."

The ghost of Julius Caesar entered Brutus' tent, causing the candle's flame to quiver.

"How badly this candle burns!" Brutus said. "Wait! Who comes here? I think it is the weakness of my eyes that shapes this monstrous apparition that comes toward me. Are you anything? Are you a god, an angel, or a devil, you who make my blood run cold and my hair stand up? Speak to me and tell me what or who you are."

"I am your evil spirit, Brutus," Caesar's ghost said.

"Why have you come to me here?"

"To tell you that you shall see me at Philippi."

"Then I shall see you again?"

"Yes, at Philippi."

Recovering his courage, Brutus said, "Why, I will see you at Philippi, then."

The ghost disappeared.

"Now that I have regained my courage, you have vanished," Brutus said. "Evil spirit, I want to talk to you!"

Brutus called, "Boy, Lucius! Varro! Claudius! Sirs, awake! Claudius!" He wanted to know if they had seen the ghost.

Still asleep and dreaming, Lucius said, "The strings, my lord, are out of tune."

"He thinks he is still playing his lute," Brutus said. "Lucius, wake up!"

"My lord?"

"Were you dreaming, Lucius?" Brutus asked. "Is that why you cried out?"

"My lord, I do not think that I cried out."

"Yes, you did," Brutus said. "Did you see anything?"

"I saw nothing, my lord."

"Go to sleep again, Lucius," Brutus said.

Then he called, "Claudius!"

To Varro, he called, "Wake up!"

"My lord?" Varro and Claudius asked together.

"Why did you cry out, sirs, in your sleep?"

"Did we, my lord?" they asked.

"Yes. Did you see anything?"

"No, my lord, I saw nothing," Varro said.

"Neither did I, my lord," Claudius said.

"Go and present my compliments to my brother Cassius. Tell him to order his troops to advance early this morning. We will follow him and his troops."

"It shall be done, my lord," Varro and Claudius replied, and then they left to carry the message to Cassius.

CHAPTER 5

— 5.1 —

On the plains of Philippi, Octavius was talking to Mark Antony. Their troops were camped on the plains.

"Now, Antony, our hopes are answered," Octavius said. "The enemy forces have made a tactical mistake. You said that the enemy would not come down from their strong defensive position, but would instead stay on the hills and upper regions. They did not do that. Their armies are close to us. They mean to challenge us at Philippi here. They are responding to our challenge even before we have made it."

"I can put myself in their place and know what they are thinking," Antony said. "I know why they are doing this. They would like to approach us from different directions and make a surprise attack against us with a show of bravery, thinking to make us believe that they are courageous, but they are not brave."

A messenger arrived and said, "Prepare yourselves, generals. The enemy marches toward us and makes a gallant show. They are wearing red vests — their bloody signs of battle — over their armor. Some action will have to be taken immediately."

"Octavius, lead your army slowly to the left side of the level field," Antony said.

"My army will take the right side of the battlefield. You and your army will take the left side," Octavius replied.

"Why are you opposing me in this urgent matter?" Antony said.

"I am not opposing you, but my army and I will take the right side of the battlefield."

Brutus, Cassius, Lucilius, Titinius, Messala, and others approached to talk to Mark Antony and Octavius before the battle began.

Brutus said, "They are willing to talk."

"Stay here, Titinius," Cassius said. "Brutus and I will talk to them."

"Mark Antony, shall we give the order to attack?" Octavius Caesar asked.

"No, Caesar, we will respond when they attack. Let you and I go forward. Their generals would have some words with us."

Octavius said to his officers, "Don't move until we give the signal."

"Words before blows," Brutus said. "Is that the way it is, countrymen?"

"We do not love words better than battle, as you do," Octavius said.

"Good words are better than bad strokes, Octavius," Brutus replied.

"To accompany your bad strokes, Brutus, you gave good words," Antony replied. "Your dagger put a hole in Caesar's heart as you cried out, 'Long live Caesar! Hail, Caesar!'"

"Antony, we do not yet know what kind of blows you will strike, but we do know that your words rob the bees around Hybla, a town in Sicily that is famous for its honey," Cassius said. "Your words leave those bees honeyless."

"But not stingless," Antony said.

"Oh, yes, and soundless, too," Brutus said. "For you have stolen their buzzing, Antony, and very wisely you threaten before you sting."

"Villains, you gave no warning before your vile daggers crashed against each other in the body of Julius Caesar," Antony replied. "You grinned like apes, and fawned like hounds, and bowed like slaves. You kissed Caesar's feet, while damned Casca, like a dog, stood behind Caesar and stabbed him in the neck. You flattered Caesar as you murdered him!"

"We are flatterers!" Cassius said. "Now, Brutus, thank yourself. Antony's tongue would not be insulting us in this way today, if you had listened to me and let us kill Antony when we killed Julius Caesar."

"Get to the point," Octavius Caesar said. "If arguing makes us sweat, settling the argument in battle will make us drip redder drops — our blood! Look, I am drawing my sword against conspirators. When do you think that I will sheathe my sword again? Not until Julius Caesar's three and thirty wounds are well avenged, or until another Caesar — me — has been killed by the swords of traitors."

"Caesar, it is impossible for you to die at the hands of traitors unless you yourself bring traitors here. We are not traitors; we are loyal to Rome," Brutus said.

"I hope that it is impossible for me to die at the hands of traitors," Octavius Caesar said. "I was not born to die on Brutus' sword."

"Even if you were the noblest of your family, young man, you could not die more honorably than on my sword," Brutus said.

"Octavius is a peevish schoolboy, unworthy of such honor," Cassius said, knowing that Octavius was only 21 years old. "He is allied with Mark Antony, who is known for partying and reveling."

"Cassius — you never change," Antony said.

"Antony, let's leave," Octavius said.

To Brutus and Cassius, Octavius said, "We hurl defiance in your teeth. If you dare fight today, come to the battlefield. If not, come when you have stomachs for fighting."

Octavius and Antony left.

Cassius said, "Why, now the wind is blowing, the swells are billowing, and the ships are floating. The storm has started, and everything is at stake."

"Lucilius!" Brutus said.

"Yes, my lord?"

"I want to speak to you."

Brutus and Lucilius talked privately.

Cassius said, "Messala!"

"Yes, my general?"

"Messala, this is my birthday; on this very day was Cassius born. Give me your hand, Messala. Be my witness that against my will, as Pompey was, am I compelled to risk everything in one battle. Pompey fought at Pharsalia against his better judgment — he was defeated. You know that I used to strongly believe in the Greek philosopher Epicurus and his teachings. He believed that omens were mere superstitions. Now I change my mind, and I partially believe in things that do presage the future. As we travelled here from Sardis, on our foremost standard — our foremost flag — two mighty eagles fell, and there they perched, gorging and feeding from our soldiers' hands. From Sardis to Philippi, they accompanied us. This morning, they flew away and are gone. And in their steads do ravens, crows, and kites — all kinds of scavenger birds — fly over our heads and look down on us, as if our corpses will soon be food for them. Their shadows seem to be a deadly canopy, under which our army lies, ready to die."

"Do not believe that this is an omen," Messala said.

"I only partially believe it," Cassius said. "I am of good spirits and resolved to face all dangers very courageously."

"That is right, Lucilius," Brutus said, ending their private conversation.

"Now, most noble Brutus," Cassius said, "may the gods today be friendly to us, so that we, lovers of peace, may live on to reach old age! But since the affairs of men are always uncertain, let us consider the worst that may befall us. If we lose this battle, then this is the very last time we shall speak together. What are you determined to do if we lose the battle?"

"As a Stoic, I blame Marcus Porcius Cato for the death that he gave himself," Brutus said. "He opposed Julius Caesar, and rather than surrender to him he committed suicide. I am not sure why, but I find it cowardly and vile to commit suicide out of fear of what may happen. I plan to be patient and accept without complaining whatever the gods send to us."

"Then, if we lose this battle, you will accept being led as a prisoner in triumph through the streets of Rome?" Cassius asked.

"No, Cassius, no," Brutus said. "Do not think, noble Roman, that Brutus will allow himself to go bound to Rome. I bear too great a mind for that — I am too proud to allow that to happen. But this day must end that work the Ides of March began. Whether we shall meet again, I do not know. Therefore, let us make our final farewells. So, farewell forever, Cassius! If we meet again, then we shall smile. If we do not meet again, then this parting was well done."

"Forever, and forever, farewell, Brutus!" Cassius said. "If we do meet again, we will smile indeed. If not, it is true that this parting was well done."

"Why, then, lead on," Brutus said. "I wish that a man might know how this day will end before it happens! But it is enough that the day will end, and then we will know the end. Let us go now."

— 5.2 —

The battle had not yet started.

Brutus gave Messala some written orders and said, "Ride, Messala, ride, and give these orders to Cassius' legions on the other side. Let them set on and fight at once because I see only faint courage in the soldiers in Octavius' army. A sudden attack by my wing will defeat them. Ride, Messala. Let all our soldiers attack now."

— 5.3 —

Later, in Cassius' part of the battlefield, Cassius and Titinius were talking.

"Look, Titinius, some of our soldiers have turned cowards and are fleeing! I myself have turned enemy to my own soldiers. This standard bearer here of mine was running away, and so I killed the coward, and took the flag from him."

"Cassius, Brutus gave the orders to attack too early," Titinius said. "Having some advantage over Octavius' army, he took it too eagerly and his soldiers began to loot, while we are surrounded by Antony's army."

Pindarus came running and said, "Run further off, my lord, run further off. Mark Antony is at your tents, my lord. Run, therefore, noble Cassius, run further off. Retreat."

"This hill is far enough away," Cassius said. "Look, Titinius. Are those my tents where I see fire?"

"Yes, they are, my lord."

"Titinius, if you are my friend, mount my horse, and ride quickly to the troops there and bring back news of whether those troops are our friends or our enemies."

"I will be here again as quickly as thought."

Titinius left.

"Go, Pindarus, get higher on that hill," Cassius ordered. "My sight has always been poor. Watch Titinius, and tell me what happens."

Pindarus climbed higher on the hill.

Cassius said to himself, "This day is the day I breathed first. This is the day that I was born. Time has come round, and where I began, there I shall end. My life has run its circle, and I will die today."

He called to Pindarus, "What do you see?"

"My lord!"

"What is happening?"

"Titinius is surrounded by horsemen who quickly ride toward him. He is riding quickly toward them. Now they are almost on him. Titinius! Now some horsemen dismount. Now, he dismounts, too. He has been captured."

Shouts rose in the air.

"Listen," Pindarus said, "The enemy soldiers are shouting for joy."

"Come down and don't look any more," Cassius said. "I am a coward because I have lived so long that I have seen my best friend captured before my eyes!"

Pindarus came down from higher on the hill.

"Come here," Cassius said. "In Parthia I took you prisoner and then I made you swear that if I did not kill you that whatever I ordered you to do you would attempt to do it. Come now, and keep your oath. Now you can earn your freedom. Take this good sword that ran through Caesar's bowels and helped to kill him — plunge this good sword into my chest. Don't talk. Don't hesitate. Here, take the hilt of the sword, and wait until I have covered my face."

Cassius covered his face with some clothing.

"Now plunge the sword into my chest."

Pindarus stabbed Cassius, who said, "Caesar, you are revenged with the sword that killed you."

Cassius died.

Pindarus said to himself, "So, I am free, yet this is not the way I wanted to gain my freedom. Cassius, I will run far from this country. I will go where no Roman shall ever take note of me."

He ran away.

Titinius, wearing a wreath of victory, and Messala rode toward Cassius' corpse.

"The armies have simply changed their positions," Messala said to Titinius. "Brutus' army defeated Octavius' army, and Antony's army defeated Cassius' army."

"This news of Brutus' victory will well comfort Cassius," Titinius said.

"Where did you leave him?" Messala asked.

"He was disconsolate and in despair with Pindarus, his slave, on this hill," Titinius said.

"Is not that he who is lying on the ground?"

"He does not lie like a living person," Titinius said. "Oh, my heart!"

"Is that Cassius?"

"No, but he was Cassius," Titinius said. "Messala, Cassius lives no more. Oh, setting Sun, just as in your red rays you will sink tonight, so in his red blood Cassius' day has set. The Sun of Rome has set! Our day is over. Clouds, the dews of evening, and dangers come. Our deeds are done! Mistrust of my success has done this deed — Cassius mistook good news for bad news and so killed himself."

"Mistrust of good success has done this deed," Messala said. "Oh, hateful error, you are the child of melancholy. You make men think thoughts that are false. Error is quickly conceived, but it kills its mother and nothing good can come from it."

"Pindarus! Where are you, Pindarus?" Titinius said.

"Seek him, Titinius," Messala said, "while I go and meet the noble Brutus, and tell him what has happened here. I may as well say that I will thrust this report into his ears because piercing steel and poisoned darts shall be as welcome to the ears of Brutus as the news of the suicide of his friend."

"Hurry, Messala," Titinius said. "I will look for Pindarus while you are gone."

Messala rode away.

"Why did you send me to your camp, brave Cassius?" Titinius said to Cassius' corpse. "Didn't I meet your friends? And didn't they put on my brows this wreath of victory, and tell me to give it to you? Didn't you hear their joyful shouts? You misunderstood everything! You mistook very good news for very bad news! But let me put this wreath of victory upon your brow. Brutus told me to give it to you, and I will do what he asked. Brutus, come quickly, and see how I respected Caius Cassius."

He took Cassius' sword and said, "Give me your permission to kill myself, gods — this is what is expected of a Roman. Come, Cassius' sword, and find Titinius' heart."

Titinius killed himself with Cassius' sword.

Messala returned with Brutus, young Cato, Strato, Volumnius, and Lucilius. Young Cato's father was Marcus Porcius Cato, who had supported Pompey and had killed himself rather than surrender to Julius Caesar. Young Cato's sister was Portia, Brutus' late wife.

"Where, Messala, does Cassius' body lie?" Brutus asked.

"Over there," Messala said. "Titinius was mourning the corpse."

"Titinius is facing upward," Brutus said.

"He is dead," young Cato said.

"Julius Caesar, you are powerful even now," Brutus said. "Your spirit walks abroad and turns our swords so that they pierce our own bodies."

"Look, noble Titinius has crowned the dead Cassius with a wreath of victory."

"Are there still two Romans living such as these?" Brutus asked. "The last of all the Romans, fare you well! It is impossible that Rome should ever breed your equals. Friends, I owe more tears to this dead man than you shall see me pay. I shall find time to mourn you properly. Cassius, I shall find time. Come, let us send his body to the nearby island of Thasos. We will not hold his funeral in our camps because it would dishearten and demoralize us. Lucilius, come, and come, young Cato, let us return to the battlefield."

He added, "Labeo and Flavius, set our troops in battle formation. It is three o'clock, and, Romans, before night falls we will try our fortunes in a second fight."

— 5.4 —

The armies were fighting each other. Brutus, Messala, Flavius, young Cato, and Lucilius and others were fighting.

"Keep fighting, countrymen," Brutus shouted. "Hold your heads up high!"

Brutus, Messala, and Flavius left to fight on another part of the battlefield.

"Who is of such bastard blood that he will not hold his head up high?" young Cato shouted. "Who will go with me? I will shout my name in the battlefield — I am the son of Marcus Cato! I am a foe to tyrants, and my country's friend! I am the son of Marcus Cato!"

Cato fought fiercely, but an opposing soldier killed him.

"And I am Brutus, Marcus Junius Brutus! I am Brutus, my country's friend!" Lucilius shouted. "Know that I am Brutus!"

Lucilius wanted Brutus to be safe. By saying that he was Brutus, he knew that the opposing soldiers who heard him would focus on him, not on the real Brutus.

He saw the corpse of young Cato and said, "Oh, young and noble Cato, are you down? Why, now you die as nobly as Titinius. And you, being Marcus Cato's son, will be honored."

One of Antony's soldiers said to Lucilius, "Surrender, or die!"

"I prefer to die," Lucilius said. "Here is some money. Take it, and kill me. I am Brutus. Kill me and win honor because you have killed me."

"We must not kill you," the soldier said. "You are nobly born."

A second soldier of Antony's shouted, "Make room for us! Get out of the way! Carry the news to Antony that Brutus has been captured."

The first soldier said, "I will tell him. Here he comes now."

Antony arrived, and the first soldier said, "Brutus has been captured, my lord."

"Where is he?" Antony asked.

"He is somewhere safe," Lucilius said. "I have been pretending to be him. Brutus is safe enough, and I assure you that no enemy shall ever take the noble

72

Brutus alive — may the gods defend him from so great a shame! When you find him, whether he is alive or dead, he will be found to be noble Brutus — he will behave in accordance with his own true and noble nature.”

“This man is not Brutus, friends,” Antony told his soldiers, “but he is, I assure you, a prize no less in worth. Keep this man safe and show him kindness. I prefer that such men be my friends than my enemies. Go and see whether Brutus is alive or dead and come to Octavius’ tent and tell us your news.”

— 5.5 —

Brutus, Dardanius, Clitus, Strato, and Volumnius knew that they had lost the battle. Strato was one of Brutus’ servants.

Brutus said, “Come here, poor friendly survivors of this battle, and last of my living friends, and rest on this rock.”

Clitus said, “Statilius showed the torchlight to us — a signal that all was going well in another part of the battle — but, my lord, he did not return to us. He must have been either captured or killed.”

“Sit down and rest, Clitus,” Brutus said. “‘Killed’ is the word most likely to be accurate. Today, killing has been fashionable. Clitus, let me speak privately to you.”

Brutus whispered to Clitus, who replied, “What, I, my lord? No, not for all the world.”

“Be quiet, then,” Brutus said. “Say no more.”

“I’ll rather kill myself than do what you asked me to do.”

Brutus went to Dardanius and said, “Listen to me.”

Brutus whispered to Dardanius, who said, “Shall I do such a deed?”

Clitus said, “Oh, Dardanius!”

Dardanius said, “Oh, Clitus!”

“What evil thing did Brutus ask you to do?”

“To kill him, Clitus. Look, he is meditating about what to do.”

“That noble vessel is so full of grief that it trickles out of his eyes,” Clitus said.

“Come here, good Volumnius,” Brutus said, “and listen to me.”

“What is it, my lord?”

“Why, this, Volumnius. The ghost of Caesar has appeared to me twice by night: once at Sardis, and, once last night here on the battlefield of Philippi. I know that my hour of death has come.”

"No, my lord," Volumnius said.

"I am sure it has, Volumnius," Brutus said. "You see how the world goes. Our enemies have beaten us back to the pit. It is much better for us to leap into the pit ourselves than to wait until they push us in. Good Volumnius, you know that we two went to school together. For the sake of our old friendship, I ask you to please hold my sword while I run on it and kill myself."

"That's not a job for a friend, my lord," Volumnius said.

Noises made it clear that enemy soldiers were approaching.

"Run, run, my lord," Clitus said to Brutus. "We can wait here no longer."

"Farewell to you; and you; and you, Volumnius. Strato, you have been asleep all this while," Brutus said. "Farewell to you, too, Strato. Countrymen, my heart rejoices that in all my life I have found only men who were true to me. I shall gain glory on this losing day — more glory than Octavius and Mark Antony shall gain with their dishonorable and vile victory. So farewell now. Brutus' tongue has almost ended its life's history. Night hangs upon my eyes, and my bones want to rest. My body has labored hard to bring me to this hour of death."

The noise of enemy soldiers grew nearer. Some of Brutus' soldiers shouted on the battlefield, "Run! Run for your lives!"

"Run, my lord, run!" Clitus pleaded.

"Go now! I will follow you," Brutus said.

Clitus, Dardanius, and Volumnius fled.

"Please, Strato, stay here by me," Brutus said. "You are a fellow with a good reputation. You have earned honor in your life. Hold then my sword, and turn away your face, while I run on my sword and kill myself. Will you do that for me, Strato?"

"Give me your hand first," Strato said.

They shook hands, and Strato said, "Farewell, my lord."

"Farewell, good Strato."

Strato held the sword firmly and turned his face to the side.

Brutus ran on his sword, fell, and said, "Caesar, now be still. I did not kill you with half so good a will as that with which I kill myself."

Brutus died.

Octavius and Mark Antony and some of their soldiers arrived with two bound prisoners: Messala and Lucilius.

"What man is that?" Octavius said, referring to Strato.

"My master's servant," Messala said. "Strato, where is Brutus, your master?"

"He is free from the bondage you are in, Messala," Strato said. "The conquerors can but make a funeral fire for him because Brutus conquered himself, and no other man but himself has gained honor from his death."

"It is fitting that Brutus should be found like this," Lucilius said. "I thank you, Brutus, because you have proved what I said to be true. I said that when Antony found Brutus, whether he is alive or dead, he would be found to be noble Brutus — he would behave in accordance with his own true and noble nature."

"Everyone who served Brutus, I will take into my service," Octavius said.

He said to Strato, "Will you join with me?"

"Yes, if Messala will recommend me to you," Strato replied.

"Recommend him, good Messala," Octavius said.

First, Messala asked, "How did my master, Brutus, die, Strato?"

"I held the sword, and he ran on it," Strato said.

"Octavius, take Strato into your service. He did the final service to my master."

Mark Antony said over Brutus' corpse, "This was the noblest Roman of them all. All the conspirators except only he did what they did out of envy of great Caesar. Brutus joined the conspirators only because he honestly believed that he was acting for the general good of all. His life was noble, and his character was such that Nature might stand up and say to all the world, 'This was a man!'"

"Let us treat him according to his virtue and excellence," Octavius said. "We will give him all respect and rites of burial. Within my tent his bones shall lie tonight with the honors due to a soldier. Order the fighting to stop, and let us return to our camp to enjoy the glories of this happy day."

NOTE

In Shakespeare's plays based on history, he collapses time. The events of *Julius Caesar* appear to take place in six days, but in reality, they took place in three years. Here are some dates:

In 48 BCE, Julius Caesar defeated Pompey at the Battle of Pharsalia.

On 17 March 45 BCE Julius Caesar defeated Pompey's sons at the Battle of Munda.

In October 45 BCE, Julius Caesar celebrated his victory over Pompey's sons in a triumphal procession in Rome. In *Julius Caesar*, Shakespeare had this triumphal procession occur on 15 February 44 BCE — the day of the Feast of Lupercal, a festival of fruitfulness and fertility.

In 44 BCE on the Ides of March (March 15), Julius Caesar was assassinated in Rome. His assassins included Caius Cassius and Marcus Junius Brutus.

In the first week of October 42 BCE, Caius Cassius committed suicide at Philippi after an engagement with the troops of Mark Antony and Octavian.

On 23 October 42 BCE, a second engagement occurred at Philippi, and Marcus Junius Brutus committed suicide.

APPENDIX A: ABOUT THE AUTHOR

It was a dark and stormy night. Suddenly a cry rang out, and on a hot summer night in 1954, Josephine, wife of Carl Bruce, gave birth to a boy — me. Unfortunately, this young married couple allowed Reuben Saturday, Josephine's brother, to name their first-born. Reuben, aka "The Joker," decided that Bruce was a nice name, so he decided to name me Bruce Bruce. I have gone by my middle name — David — ever since.

Being named Bruce David Bruce hasn't been all bad. Bank tellers remember me very quickly, so I don't often have to show an ID. It can be fun in charades, also. When I was a counselor as a teenager at Camp Echoing Hills in Warsaw, Ohio, a fellow counselor gave the signs for "sounds like" and "two words," then she pointed to a bruise on her leg twice. Bruise Bruise? Oh yeah, Bruce Bruce is the answer!

Uncle Reuben, by the way, gave me a haircut when I was in kindergarten. He cut my hair short and shaved a small bald spot on the back of my head. My mother wouldn't let me go to school until the bald spot grew out again.

Of all my brothers and sisters (six in all), I am the only transplant to Athens, Ohio. I was born in Newark, Ohio, and have lived all around Southeastern Ohio. However, I moved to Athens to go to Ohio University and have never left.

At Ohio U, I never could make up my mind whether to major in English or Philosophy, so I got a bachelor's degree with a double major in both areas, then I added a Master of Arts degree in English and a Master of Arts degree in Philosophy. Yes, I have my MAMA degree.

Currently, and for a long time to come (I eat fruits and veggies), I am spending my retirement writing books such as *Nadia Comaneci: Perfect 10*, *The Funniest People in Dance*, *Homer's* Iliad: *A Retelling in Prose*, and *William Shakespeare's* Othello: *A Retelling in Prose*.

By the way, my sister Brenda Kennedy writes romances such as *A New Beginning* and *Shattered Dreams*.

APPENDIX B: SOME BOOKS BY DAVID BRUCE

Retellings of a Classic Work of Literature

Arden of Faversham*: A Retelling*

Ben Jonson's The Alchemist: *A Retelling*

Ben Jonson's The Arraignment, or Poetaster: *A Retelling*

Ben Jonson's Bartholomew Fair: *A Retelling*

Ben Jonson's The Case is Altered: *A Retelling*

Ben Jonson's Catiline's Conspiracy: *A Retelling*

Ben Jonson's The Devil is an Ass: *A Retelling*

Ben Jonson's Epicene: *A Retelling*

Ben Jonson's Every Man in His Humor: *A Retelling*

Ben Jonson's Every Man Out of His Humor: *A Retelling*

Ben Jonson's The Fountain of Self-Love, or Cynthia's Revels: *A Retelling*

Ben Jonson's The Magnetic Lady, or Humors Reconciled: *A Retelling*

Ben Jonson's The New Inn, or The Light Heart: *A Retelling*

Ben Jonson's Sejanus' Fall: *A Retelling*

Ben Jonson's The Staple of News: *A Retelling*

Ben Jonson's A Tale of a Tub: *A Retelling*

Ben Jonson's Volpone, or the Fox: *A Retelling*

Christopher Marlowe's Complete Plays: Retellings

Christopher Marlowe's Dido, Queen of Carthage: *A Retelling*

Christopher Marlowe's Doctor Faustus: *Retellings of the 1604 A-Text and of the 1616 B-Text*

Christopher Marlowe's Edward II: *A Retelling*

Christopher Marlowe's The Massacre at Paris: *A Retelling*

Christopher Marlowe's The Rich Jew of Malta: *A Retelling*

Christopher Marlowe's Tamburlaine, Parts 1 and 2: *Retellings*

Dante's Divine Comedy: *A Retelling in Prose*

Dante's Inferno: *A Retelling in Prose*

Dante's Purgatory: *A Retelling in Prose*

Dante's Paradise: *A Retelling in Prose*

The Famous Victories of Henry V: *A Retelling*

From the Iliad *to the* Odyssey: *A Retelling in Prose of Quintus of Smyrna's* Posthomerica

George Chapman, Ben Jonson, and John Marston's Eastward Ho! *A Retelling*

George Peele's The Arraignment of Paris: *A Retelling*

George Peele's The Battle of Alcazar: *A Retelling*

George's Peele's David and Bathsheba, and the Tragedy of Absalom: *A Retelling*

George Peele's Edward I: *A Retelling*

George Peele's The Old Wives' Tale: *A Retelling*

William Shakespeare's 38 Plays: Retellings in Prose
William Shakespeare's 1 Henry IV, aka Henry IV, Part 1: *A Retelling in Prose*
William Shakespeare's 2 Henry IV, aka Henry IV, Part 2: *A Retelling in Prose*
William Shakespeare's 1 Henry VI, aka Henry VI, Part 1: *A Retelling in Prose*
William Shakespeare's 2 Henry VI, aka Henry VI, Part 2: *A Retelling in Prose*
William Shakespeare's 3 Henry VI, aka Henry VI, Part 3: *A Retelling in Prose*
William Shakespeare's All's Well that Ends Well: *A Retelling in Prose*
William Shakespeare's Antony and Cleopatra: *A Retelling in Prose*
William Shakespeare's As You Like It: *A Retelling in Prose*
William Shakespeare's The Comedy of Errors: *A Retelling in Prose*
William Shakespeare's Coriolanus: *A Retelling in Prose*
William Shakespeare's Cymbeline: *A Retelling in Prose*
William Shakespeare's Hamlet: *A Retelling in Prose*
William Shakespeare's Henry V: *A Retelling in Prose*
William Shakespeare's Henry VIII: *A Retelling in Prose*
William Shakespeare's Julius Caesar: *A Retelling in Prose*
William Shakespeare's King John: *A Retelling in Prose*
William Shakespeare's King Lear: *A Retelling in Prose*
William Shakespeare's Love's Labor's Lost: *A Retelling in Prose*
William Shakespeare's Macbeth: *A Retelling in Prose*
William Shakespeare's Measure for Measure: *A Retelling in Prose*
William Shakespeare's The Merchant of Venice: *A Retelling in Prose*
William Shakespeare's The Merry Wives of Windsor: *A Retelling in Prose*
William Shakespeare's A Midsummer Night's Dream: *A Retelling in Prose*
William Shakespeare's Much Ado About Nothing: *A Retelling in Prose*
William Shakespeare's Othello: *A Retelling in Prose*
William Shakespeare's Pericles, Prince of Tyre: *A Retelling in Prose*
William Shakespeare's Richard II: *A Retelling in Prose*
William Shakespeare's Richard III: *A Retelling in Prose*
William Shakespeare's Romeo and Juliet: *A Retelling in Prose*
William Shakespeare's The Taming of the Shrew: *A Retelling in Prose*
William Shakespeare's The Tempest: *A Retelling in Prose*
William Shakespeare's Timon of Athens: *A Retelling in Prose*
William Shakespeare's Titus Andronicus: *A Retelling in Prose*
William Shakespeare's Troilus and Cressida: *A Retelling in Prose*
William Shakespeare's Twelfth Night: *A Retelling in Prose*
William Shakespeare's The Two Gentlemen of Verona: *A Retelling in Prose*
William Shakespeare's The Two Noble Kinsmen: *A Retelling in Prose*
William Shakespeare's The Winter's Tale: *A Retelling in Prose*